WILLIAM BELL

Aladdin Paperbacks

New York London Toronto Sydney Singapore

ROCKFORD PUBLIC LIBRARY

If you purchased this book without a cover you should be aware that this book is stolen property. It was reported as "unsold and destroyed" to the publisher and neither the author nor the publisher has received any payment for this "stripped book."

First Aladdin Paperbacks edition December 2000

Copyright © 1998 by William Bell

Aladdin Paperbacks
An imprint of Simon & Schuster
Children's Publishing Division
1230 Avenue of the Americas
New York, NY 10020

All rights reserved, including the right of reproduction in whole or in part in any form.

Also available in a Simon & Schuster Books for Young Readers hardcover edition

Designed by Paul Zakris
The text for this book was set in 12-point Janson Text.

Printed and bound in the United States of America

10 9 8 7 6 5 4 3 2 1

The Library of Congress has cataloged the hardcover edition as follows:

Bell, William, 1945-
Zack / William Bell.—1st U.S. ed.
p. cm.
Summary: The son of a Jewish father and black mother, high school senior Zack has never been allowed to meet his mother's family, but after doing a research project on a former slave, he travels from his home in Canada to Natchez, Mississippi, to find his grandfather.
ISBN: 0-689-82248-0 (hc.)
[1. Racially mixed people—Fiction. 2. Prejudices—Fiction. 3. Blacks—Canada—Fiction. 4. Canada—Fiction.] I. Title.
PZ7.B41187Zac 1999 [Fic]—dc21 98-6690 CIP AC
ISBN: 0-689-82529-3 (Aladdin pbk.)

FOR TING-XING YE

like gold to aery thinness beat

PART ONE

"You can never place your foot into the same river twice," my dad often reminded me, quoting some ancient Greek philosopher with an unpronounceable name. I wondered as I scraped the sole of my high-top on the spade's edge if the same wisdom applied to stepping in dog droppings. Between our new house and the row of cedars that fringed the river, the dry brown grass was littered with revolting little piles of fossilized puppy poop that had magically appeared as the snow thawed.

Scooping dog doo-doo pretty much summed up the way I felt about moving to that place. The house itself was all right. Under torture I would have admitted that it was better than our cramped two-bedroom apartment in the city. I had a decent room on the second floor with a big window looking over the yard, but that wasn't much consolation. I was used to going to school through the rumble and snarl of traffic, sidewalks teeming with people rushing past restaurants, pool halls, video arcades, and head shops. I had traveled on a city bus jammed with faces of every color and humming with languages from around the world. Now each morning I stood like a stump at the end of our unpaved driveway waiting for the big yellow monster to swallow me up and transport me to Boredom High School. I had been dragged from a major street in the biggest city in the country to the edge of the known universe, a rural route in Garafraxa Township—the name sounded like an incurable skin disease—with a chicken farm at the dead end, on the outskirts of a no-place village called Fergus where, as near as I could tell, the locals' idea of a good time was trying on gloves at the department store or watching the blue light revolve on the top of the snowplow.

There was nothing funny about being the only child of two stubborn parents who had decided to leave the city and do the pioneer thing among the trees. I had visions of alfalfa sprouts and seeds for lunch, Mom weaving her own cloth, Dad dressed in a tartan bush shirt and faded jeans, chopping kindling and spitting black tobacco juice.

"It's a great opportunity for your dad," my mother had told me a year ago, after she dropped the bomb. "He'll be chair of the department."

"Your mom has never liked the city," Dad had said in a different conversation. "She can set up a recording studio in the house, like she's always wanted. And have a garden."

Two against one. What the kid wanted didn't count; he didn't get a vote. For months I ranted, sulked, and threw things around my room. On purpose I flunked two courses. I ran away for three days. We moved anyway. And now, here I was in the backyard, Zack Lane, Canine Feces Remover.

I knew from the sour smell that Jenkins had sneaked up behind me just as the download was completed, and that he had seen me eject the diskette and slip it into my shirt pocket.

"Let's have it, Zack," he commanded, his voice betraying a hint of triumph.

I clicked the mouse and blanked the screen. "Um, what's wrong, sir?"

"You know what."

"It's just my own personal disk," I said. "It's, you know, confidential."

"Nice try."

"I can explain."

"I'm not interested. Let's have it."

I took the diskette out of my pocket and passed it back over my shoulder.

"Stick around at the end of the period."

Outside the dirty window of the computer lab on the second floor of the school a fine rain fell out of a low gray sky. Our geography class had spent the last hour pulling down weather maps from some satellite or other so we could watch bright green meteorological patterns flowing amoeba-like across the blue map on our screens. That is, most of us had. On one side of me a skinny guy who had just returned from a three-day suspension was painting hearts with initials in them on his binder with white correction fluid. On the other, a girl sporting purple hyperextended false fingernails urgently explained to her friend why she "absolutely hated" her own hair.

I already knew it was raining so I connected to the Internet and surfed for certain information I was after. It had taken me most of the period to find some good stuff, almost oblivious to the *clickety click* of keyboards and mice and the hum of conversation.

Going "off task" hadn't been difficult because Jenkins had spent most of the period with his sleeves rolled up, hunched over his cluttered desk marking tests and pumping out the BO. Short, rotund, and an early victim of pattern baldness, he was best known for the stale body odor that enveloped him like a damp fog.

As my classmates filed out of the room, some casting curious glances my way, Jenkins tightened the tie he had worn for five days running and slipped on an old tweed jacket.

"Meet me in Ms. O'Neil's office after last class, Zack. And bring your computer-use contract with you."

An hour and a half later I plowed through the noisy chaos of the halls to the principal's office, more irritated than worried. O'Neil would probably give me a reprimand and revoke my computer privileges. Unauthorized downloads were treated seriously by the school. I didn't blame them. There was all sorts of disgusting crap available on the Net and the school didn't want us finding, seeing, or downloading it and corrupting ourselves. If you got caught, you'd lose your log-in and could only use computers for word processing and spreadsheets and stuff—unless you had a friend who would let you use his log-in, which I didn't. The truth was that the school had about as much success controlling Net access as it did preventing the drug trade.

When I got to the reception area and reported to the secretary I was ushered into O'Neil's inner office as if I held expensive tickets to a concert. O'Neil was a middle-aged woman, tall and slender with graying hair, casually dressed in slacks and a white blouse. I hadn't had dealings with her since she registered me on my arrival months before. At that time she had been all smiles. Now she frowned with that look of momentary concern that teachers are good at.

She sat in a leather chair behind an expansive wooden desk. Jenkins occupied a chair beside her.

"Put your contract on the desk and take a seat, Zack," O'Neil said, then picked up the phone and punched in a number.

I tossed the paper onto her desk blotter and lowered myself into a chair. Jenkins looked out the window, then examined his knuckles. The three of us sat like that for a while. O'Neil finished her conversation and put down the phone. A second later it buzzed. She picked it up, listened, then said "Fine, Laura. Send him in."

The principal rose from her chair, eyes on the door. When it opened her eyebrows rose in surprise. She shot a quick look at me, rapidly composed herself, smiled and purred, "Mr. Lane? Come in, please."

She had, naturally, assumed my father would be black. Surprise, surprise, Ms. O., I thought.

My father walked into the room with the graceful ease of an athlete. He was wearing a cardigan over a white cotton shirt, tan cords, and loafers—his usual academic garb. When the introductions were made and hands were shaken he took the remaining chair. He looked vaguely irritated, the way he did if I interrupted him when he was writing a paper or making notes in his cramped, neat handwriting, deep in concentration, surrounded by stacks of books and periodicals with slips of yellow paper sticking out from between the pages.

Bringing my father in was going a little too far, but I kept my mouth shut. It might be fun, I thought, to see how this little drama plays out.

"Mr. Lane," O'Neil began, her composure regained, "we've called you in because we feel we have a rather serious problem on our hands."

She paused to heighten the drama. Slowly, Jenkins's odoriferous presence made itself evident. He studied his knuckles some more. My father crossed his legs, ankle on knee, and fiddled with his shoelace.

O'Neil removed a diskette from her desk drawer and placed it on her desk as if it was Macbeth's bloody dagger. Nodding toward the computer notebook on the corner of her desk, she said, "I'd like you to see the material that your son captured from the Internet this afternoon when he was supposed to be . . . what was the lesson today, Mr. Jenkins?"

"Er, weather patterns," Jenkins replied solemnly. "Through the satellite link."

O'Neil popped the disk into the laptop and turned it so Dad could see the screen. She scrolled slowly through the pages, giving him lots of time to get the picture.

The first page showed the front of a pamphlet. *The Jewish Conspiracy: The Truth Will Out!!!* by Ernst Krupp.

"Significant name," my father muttered, drawing a blank look from O'Neil. I had no idea what he meant either, but I was used to him making cryptic comments when something going on around him connected with something he was thinking about.

Next on the screen came a photo of a middle-aged man with thick gray hair and a florid complexion, wearing some kind of military cap with a logo on it. He stood in the center of a small crowd and someone was holding a megaphone to his mouth, which was wide open. It was summer, and trees almost hid the courthouse behind him. *Mr. Krupp tells all in his trial*, the caption under the picture read. The following pages of dense print were headed *The Lie About the Holocaust That Never Happened!!*

"You get the idea," O'Neil said, removing the diskette and shutting down the laptop. She closed the lid firmly.

"Ms. O'Neil, I'm not sure I understand why you've

called me away from my work," my father said calmly. "You said something on the phone about Zack breaking a computer-use contract—"

O'Neil seemed put out that Dad hadn't raged and foamed at the mouth when he'd seen the stuff I'd downloaded. "Well, yes. We ask that all students sign a contract before they're issued a password and log-in. The contract requires—"

"I'm familiar with the concept. We have the same policy at the university."

"Indeed. Then you'll agree with our rule against accessing or downloading material of an obscene or hateful nature. Zack copied this . . . this *material* on the sly. It's obviously neo-Nazi garbage. Wouldn't you agree?"

"Certainly."

"To be frank, Mr. Lane, we're always worried when we see this kind of thing. Aside from Zack's own opinions"—she spat out the word like a piece of rotten meat—"which, I suppose, he has a right to, I have the school's reputation to consider. I don't want the community to think that hate literature originated in this building."

Dad's voice was still calm and reasonable, a sign that he was getting angry. "Has anyone asked Zack why he wanted this literature?"

"I got it for you, Dad."

Silence. Jenkins and O'Neil stared intently at my father, probably imagining him to be an aging skinhead who had recruited his son to his evil doings.

"I thought as much," Dad said. He turned to me, a

why-did-you-get-me-into-this-mess look on his face. "You shouldn't have done it, Zack. I appreciate it; you know that. But now you're going to lose your privileges here."

"Let me see if I understand this," O'Neil cut in, fire in her eyes and ice in her voice. "Your son has acquired fascist hate literature on your behalf and it's okay with you? A load of anti-Semitic—"

"I'm a Jew, Ms. O'Neil," Dad said.

For the second time, silence fell, and so did O'Neil's jaw. Jenkins looked as if he was in the grip of a tremendous gas pain. He took another tour of his knuckles.

"But," the principal spluttered, and she almost said it. I could practically see the words on her lips—You don't look Jewish. Her blush showed through the makeup.

Dad's diplomatic smile made a rare appearance. "Ms. O'Neil, I'm an instructor at the university. My specialty is contemporary social history—a sort of oxymoron, I know. Zack was just hoping to bring home material he thought I might be interested in. I can assure you he is just as offended by it as you."

"Um, I see . . ."

"If you'll forgive me for saying so," he went on, "I think that if someone had simply asked Zack what he was up to, this misunderstanding could have been avoided."

"Well." O'Neil shot a withering glance at Jenkins, who was now fiddling with his tie. "You're quite right. I'm sorry we've troubled you." She straightened up in her chair and cleared her throat. "Considering the circumstances, we'll overlook Zack's transgression and reinstate his log-in."

My father rose from his chair. "That won't be necessary. Zack broke the rules, so he should be treated like anyone else."

Dad shook hands with the principal and Jenkins again and left the office. I followed him out and he said a quick good-bye and headed for the parking lot.

Throughout that ridiculous little one-act play I had felt like a piece of furniture. But I was used to it—being on the outside of things. It was nothing new.

My mother loved any kind of growing thing—except me, I sometimes felt—and my father loved my mother. By some kind of weird equation these two facts, when added, equaled me with a shovel in my hand and a job to do. The former owner's dog's gifts to the ecosystem had been collected and buried a few days before—by me, naturally—so I marched dutifully to the spot Mom had picked on the left side of the yard next to the wooden fence, where the land began its gentle slope to the river, and began to dig holes for three lilac bushes. Mom had given me very specific instructions on how deep and how far apart these excavations should be.

"You get the ground ready," she had told me, "I'll plant the lilacs, a white one and two purple."

"Then can I use the truck?"

"When your dad and I get home."

When lunchtime came I had dug one hole, collected a wheelbarrow full of various-size stones, raised a blister on my left palm, and stabbed myself twice in the foot with the spade. Time for a break. I stretched the kinks out of my back and plodded toward the house, my eyes peeled for wayward piles of digested dog food, and went into the kitchen. I popped open a can of iced tea and built a monster sandwich of sliced beef, cheese, pepperoni, mayonnaise, and mustard on rye. Perched on a stool at the counter, I gazed out the kitchen window as I ate, admiring the results of my labor. Over the fast-flowing Grand River the sky was clear and a light breeze stirred the cedars.

By midafternoon I had excavated a second hole and shoved another wheelbarrow full of stones down the riverbank, scaring up a pair of ducks that had been floating peacefully in the current. The third and last hole was easy going for the first twenty inches or so, then the spade clanged against a rock. I dug around the obstruction, hauled it out and tossed it into the wheelbarrow. Unlike the others, it was black with carbon and soot and crusted with damp, powdery mortar. So were the next half dozen. Someone must have made a fire pit here, I thought, cursing whoever it was for their lack of consideration. I cleared the loose dirt from the hole and decided to go down another six inches or so, widen the cavity, and call it quits. I stabbed the spade into the soil, stepped on the flange, jounced my full weight on it, and heard the edge of the spade grind against something hard. Another rock, I thought. It clanked against the side of the wheelbarrow when I threw it in, but it wasn't a stone.

The caked dirt fell away easily under the pressure of my fingers. I carried the heavy object to the side of the house and washed it under the hose. The remaining soil dissolved away from an ax head, caked with rust, the handle long since rotted from the slot, the edge dull and rounded. I hadn't seen many ax heads in my city-boy life, but I knew from the unusual shape that this one was very, very old. I turned it over in my hands a few times, then dropped it by the kitchen door on my way back to the hole. The day wasn't a total loss, but it was close.

My next spade thrust brought a hollow *thump*. Now what? I got to my knees and picked up a triangle-shaped splinter of wood, bright on one side. I scooped dirt away with my hand, uncovering the corner of a box of some kind.

A half hour of painstaking soil removal passed, during which my interest perked with every handful of dirt I removed, before I was able to lift the box from the hole—carefully, because the wood was so soft with rot it almost fell apart in my hands. About the size of a shoe box, it had mortised corners and a lid that resisted my careful attempts to pry it off. I jogged to the house and returned with a kitchen knife, the ache in my back forgotten. I ran the blade along the dirt-clogged space between the lid and the sides of the box, working the soil loose, and finally the top broke free.

My heart quickened when I looked inside. Two rolls of what was once white leather but was now stained and faded lay in the moldy bottom of the box. I tried to unroll one but the leather began to crack and break apart. I laid the two objects on the grass.

Wrapped in ancient oily material I thought at first was cloth but turned out to be greasy leather were two

Cs of rusted iron about half an inch thick. One end of each C was bent back on itself to form a small circle that loosely linked it to the other piece. The free end of each C had an elongated box-shaped loop on it. Held together, the two half rings made a circle about eight inches in diameter. I had no idea what I was holding in my hands.

In a corner of the box lay a small skin pouch, pulled tight with a rawhide drawstring. The material tore like wet paper when I pulled it open, and a nugget the size of my pinkie finger end plopped down into the hole. I picked it up and bounced it in the palm of my hand. It was bronze in color, heavy, and hard—some kind of metal, forged into a small ball.

I wonder if it's—Then I laughed at myself. What a loser I was, getting mildly excited by a useless old wooden box with strange junk in it, so bored living in that dull village that I'd grasp at anything for a little thrill.

It was then that I heard our truck pull into the driveway. The engine raced and died. A door opened and slammed shut, followed by another. I dropped the nugget into the box, replaced the straps and iron, picked up the box and walked quickly to the kitchen. As I was gingerly pulling a plastic supermarket bag over my "buried treasure" I heard the front door open. I sprinted upstairs, dashed into my room and shoved the bag under my bed.

Dad met me at the bottom of the stairs.

"Hi, Zack. How's the farming?"

"Very exciting, Dad. I found an old ax head."

Mom put two fat bags with "Fergus Nursery" printed on the sides down on the kitchen table. "My son the anthropologist," she said.

"Archaeologist, Mom."

"Whatever."

Probably because he felt guilty that I'd gotten into trouble at school on his behalf the week before, Dad let me use the truck after supper one night without the usual intensive begging on my part and the lame excuses on his. It was a three-year-old Toyota five-speed, small, gutless, and in every sense a base model. Once I was away from the house I threw an old PUBB tape (the Practically Unknown Blues Band) into the deck, cranked it up, and headed for town with music booming out of the speakers and warm spring air flowing in the windows. I pulled down the visor against the slanting rays of the sun and rolled down the main street of Fergus. There were a few kids hanging around outside the Rhett Butler Restaurant and sitting on the front steps of the old stone library, smoking and getting in people's way.

In the blink of an eye I passed through town and continued west on a two-lane named City Road 18, solid proof that the founders of the town, who according to the sign were all Scots, had exhausted their imaginations once they had used up the names of princes, kings, queens, and saints. I was soon in Elora, where, if it was possible, even less was happening than in Fergus, and followed the signs to Elora Gorge Park.

Picnic tables were stacked under bare trees and chained together; rusted barbecues waited empty and cold for warmer weather to bring the families out. I drove through the park along narrow gravel roadways until I spotted two cars pulled up beside a stand of evergreens. Five kids stood around a fire, three guys and two girls with their backs to me. A couple of them I recognized from Jenkins's geography class.

I turned down my radio and stopped the truck.

"Hi, Colin," I yelled.

He was a tall, lanky blond guy with bad zits and, according to school legend, the best jump shot in the league. I didn't know him very well.

"Hey, Zack," he called back, "how's it goin'?"

"Great."

Somebody said something I couldn't hear and a couple of them laughed. One of the girls turned around; it was Jen. She sat behind me in homeroom and had shown me around on the first day, and by the time she had left me to go to another class, I had practically fallen in love with her. She had a compact build and an open, friendly face framed with thick auburn hair. Her eyes were deep brown, direct and honest. Jen was a far cry from the usual simpering eye-batters or brash loudmouths who thought you had to talk—and sometimes dress—like a truck driver to be taken seriously. She seemed unconventional, her own person. I had hoped I'd find her there because she had mentioned once that she and some of her friends hung out at the park.

The two guys with Colin I didn't know, but I guessed from their blue numbered tank tops that they wore in spite of the chilling air that they were b-ball players too.

"Hey, man, got any beer?" one of them yelled.

The second girl still hadn't turned around, so I couldn't tell if I knew her.

"No, but I can get some," I said without thinking.

The two tank tops let out a cheer halfway between a whoop and a snarl. "All *right!*"

"See you in a few minutes," I said, and started the truck. I pulled out, spraying gravel and watching them in my rearview mirror. Four of them turned back to their conversation. Jen watched me leave. An encouraging sign, I hoped.

I seemed to do that a lot—let my mouth get ahead of my brain. After the first flash of warmth that came with thinking they would let me join their party, I was stuck with backing up my brag. I didn't even like beer. But my dad did, once in a while. I headed home, hoping he'd have some stored in the overflow fridge in the garage and that I'd be able to lift it without my parents hearing me come back.

Twenty minutes later I barreled into the park, a twelve-pack of Molson's beside me on the seat. The party had heated up. The doors of both cars had been thrown open, both radios tuned to the same medium rock station, and five voices were locked in competition with the pounding music. The fire roared. I parked the truck and, beer under my arm, walked casually toward the group.

"Hey, an angel of mercy!" Colin crowed. "With the ticket of admission in his hands."

I set the box on the hood of one of the cars. "Help yourself," I invited.

Colin and one of the others, tall, bony, and freckled, dug in, muttering, "Thanks, man." They moved away some distance and began to toss a football back and forth after setting their beers down on the ground. I carried four cans to the fire.

The third guy wore a school jacket over his tank top, flannel warm-up shorts, and unlaced high-tops. He was shorter and heavier than the other two, with black hair and a nose that probably earned him a lot of cruel remarks when he was a kid. The girl wore a scowl on her pinched features and hunched her shoulders under her bulky sweater, as if she was freezing.

"Hi, Jen," I said, passing beers around.

"Hi, Zack. Meet Dave."

We shook hands. He had an iron grip and squeezed my hand as hard as he could, an immature guy thing that always made me laugh inside. I let my hand go limp and rolled my fingers together, a trick I learned a long time ago. Dave smirked.

"And this is my cousin Kirsten," Jen continued. "She's from Detroit. She's visiting us for a few days."

Kirsten was taller than Jen, with ash-blond hair that almost looked unbleached, and lots of makeup. Her nose stud winked in the waning light.

I popped open my beer, releasing a cascade of foam that poured over my hand. Cool move, Zack, I thought.

"Hi, Kirsten," I said. "How are things in Detroit?"

She looked me straight in the eye. "White," she sneered, and glanced away.

My breath caught in my throat, as if she had punched me in the gut.

Dave gave out a derisive laugh. Jen clapped her hand to her mouth, vainly trying to trap a giggle as her eyes saucered in surprise.

I felt the rage begin to build and my limbs quivered with the rush of adrenaline. I swallowed as my heartbeat climbed. A white rope of foam burst upward as my beer can hit the ground at my feet.

I turned, walked slowly to the truck, felt their eyes crawling on my back as I opened the door and got in. I started the engine, put the truck in gear, and drove away.

There are all kinds of words to describe someone like me, and every one of them pisses me off. I am "of varied racial origin," a blend, an alloy, a hybrid; a cross- or half-breed [or -caste]; a Créole, a double quadroon, a double-double-octaroon. Hell, I guess I'm a doubloon. How about a mulatto? That's a Spanish word and it means mule, for God's sake, half horse, half donkey, and unable to reproduce itself. I'm the result of "miscegenation"—sounds like an antibiotic, not the coming together of "two persons of different race." In my case, a Jew and a black.

But I don't look like a Jewish Negro or a black Jew. I look like a black. I am of average height, of average build, with wiry hair that I wear very short, and very dark skin. Talk about an identity crisis.

So when Jen's cousin from Detroit slammed me with her vicious remark I was shocked but not surprised. Growing up in Toronto, I was familiar with racial slurs directed by all the races at all the other races. Nobody was exempt. My old school in the city had been added to over the years until it was composed of three wings, with three major hallways. A-wing "belonged" to the blacks, B to the whites, and C to the browns—kids of Pakistani, Indian, or Sikh descent—and it was not wise to get caught in the wrong place at the wrong time, or to use the wrong doorway coming into the school.

The administration had long since given up trying to stop the turf wars and purposely distributed lockers according to race. There was a race committee—cool name, isn't it?—made up of teachers and students, and it held a lot of meetings that accomplished very little. The whole operation was maximally stupid. While classes were on, the unwritten law of territory was suspended and we all moved freely as we slouched to and from biology or English or math, shop or the resource center. But before and after classes, and at lunchtime, each piece of turf was enclosed by invisible boundaries. Even the doorways were guarded like border checkpoints and nobody, including many of the teachers, dared to venture outside the safe zones.

The system, I suppose, worked well. There were fights, but not that many. The way I saw it, the whites, browns, and blacks lived in an atmosphere of tense coexistence, while the Asians minded their own business and knocked off most of the scholarships.

The only, and I mean only, thing I liked about my new school—and this will sound weird—was that almost every student there was white, with surnames like McClintock and Stewart, Carroll and Stanhope. The collective faces at an assembly looked like a pan of homogenized milk. I had had no trouble in the short time I'd been there. I was able almost to relax. Until Jen's cousin woke me up.

I drove home, way over the speed limit.

My parents met when Mom, just starting out as a performer, was playing a blues festival at the University of Toronto. Dad was a student there and one of the organizers of the event, although he knew little about music. They started going out together regularly. Mom recognized she had a weird one on her hands when Dad showed up in Ottawa six months after they met and stood in the snow outside her window singing love songs at the top of his lungs, pelted by the sleet, claiming he wouldn't go away until she said she'd marry him.

"He was singing off-key, those musical wallpaper songs you hear on the pablum FM stations," Mom told me one time. "I said I'd marry him just to shut him up."

In spite of what Dad thought, my mother wasn't beautiful. Her nose—which I had inherited, lucky me—was a little too prominent and broad, the curved nostrils too wide. But she was pretty, with velvety black unblemished skin, big eyes, and a deep honey-smooth voice. She was fairly tall and slender, with long fingers, strong as steel from playing the guitar. And she always, always had on a pair of big gold hoop earrings.

And Dad, well, *ordinary* is the best word. He had a medium ex-athlete's build, curly black hair and brown eyes.

"I met a lot of very intelligent guys," Mom had told me. "And a few men who were kind and good, but your dad was the only one who put them both together."

Obviously, race wasn't an issue with Mom and Dad. My father didn't make much of his origins. He didn't go to synagogue and never suggested Mom or I should. It seemed like he didn't care much about the Laws, and the whole idea of kosher food was nonsense to him. Which made for some interesting discussions at my grandparents' house.

I can't remember how old I was when I asked him, "Am I a Jew, Dad?"

"I suppose so," he said. "Do you want to be?"

"Yeah."

"Okay, you're a Jew."

For her part, Mom would get very angry when she was billed as "one of Canada's foremost black performers."

"What's black got to do with it?" she would rant. "I'm a musician."

She didn't like it when people called jazz and the blues black music. "Tell that to Bill Evans," she would demand. "Benny Goodman's gonna be surprised too."

They met, married, and had me. Which was, I felt when I was old enough to be aware of such things, fine for them. They had ignored the problem and passed it on to their baby boy.

Unless you were heavily into the blues there was no reason why you would have heard of my mother, Etta Lane, who had a small but loyal following in Canada and the States, hard-core believers who liked to sit in dark clubs for hours and listen to her coax the blues from an acoustic guitar as she sang deep and smooth as a river. For as long as I could remember she had been teaching me her art, and now I was good enough to back her up sometimes. She was away from home a fair amount, with all the gigs she could handle. A year before we moved, a song she wrote and recorded, "South on 61," got a lot of radio play and made her a few bucks (and helped her and Dad buy the new house and move away from the city). It was about a woman who lived in a frozen ghetto and one day decided to head south to find her roots in the Mississippi Delta. Back in the late forties and fifties, thousands and thousands of blacks turned their backs on the worn-out farms they had sharecropped for generations and went up Highway 61 to industrial jobs in the cities of the North. It was one of the biggest migrations in human history.

Mom's song was ironic, though, or maybe a daydream, because she has told me countless times that she'd never "go back" to the small town where her family lived before they too moved to Chicago, where she was born. My grandmother died when Mom was three and her dad had gone home after he retired from a truck-parts factory. Mom hadn't seen him since she moved to Canada. I had never been told why. I'd never so much as seen a picture of him or heard his voice. I had always felt I was missing something, not having any contact with the American side of my family.

"Do I have cousins down there?" I asked her once.

"Yes."

"Aunts and uncles, the whole thing?"

"Well, that's where cousins come from, Zack," she replied with irritation.

"Why don't we go and see them? How come we don't get any Christmas or Hanukkah cards from them? Or send them any? How come—?"

"Go on out and play, Mr. Nosy. Mom has work to do." And she picked up her twelve-string, chasing me off with loud complicated jazz chords. Family was something Mom did not want to discuss. Ever.

My grandparents lived in a ramshackle two-story house with a big sunroom across the back, on a quiet tree-flanked street in the west end of the city. They had bought the place when they were young—so long ago, Grandma always claimed, that it had been the only house on the street, surrounded by apple orchards. Over the years the city had grown toward it and eventually enveloped it.

Grandpa Lane had driven a taxi since he and my grandmother had moved to Toronto from Winnipeg, and after they had scrimped and saved for some years they bought some used radio equipment, hired another guy who used his own car, and became the Shoreline Taxi Company, a strange title, since their house was at least half a mile from Lake Ontario. Dad had grown up with the crackle and static of the dispatcher's radio in his ears, Grandma being the dispatcher. Now they were retired and owned a couple of duplexes that Grandpa seemed happy to supervise and keep in repair.

Because of his years behind the wheel, Grandpa had firm opinions about automobiles and he shared these views every chance he got.

"I'll never know why you bought a pickup truck in the first place," he shouted at Dad from the front steps, shaking his head in mock wonder. "And one of those dinky foreign ones there's hardly room for you and your lunch in the cab, never mind your wife and son. Who, by the way, if he gets any bigger, won't fit even in the box!"

"Hi, Dad," my father said, shaking his head and climbing out.

I got out the other side and Mom slid along the seat to follow.

"Hello, Paul," she called from the driveway. "Hi, Mae."

"Never mind 'Hello'!" Grandpa thundered. "Come up here and give us a hug."

Grandpa was not tall but he was wide and still strong, with heavily muscled arms and wide powerful hands, and when he hugged Mom I thought he'd break her. With a head of thick white hair and a florid complexion, he radiated energy and good health.

Grandma was a contrast. Where he stood like an oak on the porch in baggy pants held up with red suspenders, a short-sleeved shirt with his reading glasses stuck in the pocket, she was a few inches taller, straight, slender, and soft-spoken, wearing a sky-blue dress, her hair stylishly short.

"It's good to see you, dear," she said as she too embraced my mother. "I heard your highway song on the radio again this morning."

It was my turn to be mauled. Grandpa almost broke my ribs and Grandma kissed me, murmuring, "If you get any handsomer I'll leave this old fool and chase after you myself."

I liked their house. The furniture was old and the rugs threadbare, but it was comfortable and inviting. I liked to visit my grandparents too. Normally. But when we were at the dinner table and everyone had a share of roast chicken, mashed potatoes, corn, and broccoli—I passed on the broccoli even after a propaganda lecture from Grandma about the wonderful things it would do for my health, pointing out that Dad hadn't taken any either—I found out that food wasn't the only thing on the menu.

The four of them ambushed me. It started out with a question from Grandma that was so uncasually casual, alarm bells went off.

"How is your new school, Zachariah?"

Grandpa's stare bore down on me like a runaway train. Mom nonchalantly scooped up a forkful of potato but didn't raise it to her mouth. Dad, who hated confrontation, was suddenly fascinated with the wallpaper.

"Okay, I guess," I answered. Be noncommittal, I told myself, hoping I could somehow get out of the coming interrogation.

"Have you adapted all right?" Grandma asked in a very nonthreatening tone. "It must be hard, going to a new school, making new friends."

"Yeah, it is."

Especially when the school is in a town the size of a tenth-rate golf course and the students know more about horses and fertilizer than good music or cool clothes.

"How are your marks?" Never famous for his patience, Grandpa got right to the point.

"Not so good," I said, aware that I was about to enter a contest with the odds stacked at four to one, a little steamed at my parents for setting me up. They knew I loved my grandparents and would do anything for them.

Grandpa put down his knife and fork. He took a few gulps from his water glass. "Listen, Zack," he began in a tone that he almost never used with me, "your education is the most important thing you have. Nowadays, without good schooling, a person can't amount to anything."

"You did okay," I countered, earning a scowl from my mother.

"What okay? A taxi driver? Working twelve hours a day? Putting up with drunks and whores in the middle of the—"

"Paul!" Grandma cried.

"All right, all right, sorry, dear. But you get my drift, Zack. That's no life. You don't want that. You can learn. You're a smart kid. Look at your dad, a university teacher. And your mom, a wonderful musician you can hear her on the radio."

I didn't bother to point out that Mom had left school after grade twelve. He'd have told me she had studied music for years, worked as hard as a one-armed wallpaper hanger—his favorite and corniest expression—and he'd have been right. But I hated it when he criticized me. I felt like I was letting him down.

"I know what's going on here," I said, looking at

Grandma because my grandfather could always stare me down, no contest. "Mom and Dad got you to hassle me about my marks. But if you want to know why I'm flunking, ask them."

Savagely, I attacked a chicken leg, slashing the meat off the bone while the silence pressed in on me.

"Listen, Zack," Grandpa began again after a few moments had passed. "You're going to let this beat you? You didn't want to move away from the city, your friends, so you're punishing your parents by flunking out? I don't say it's no hardship for you, okay. Okay?" he said again when I didn't answer.

"Okay."

"All right. It's tough on you. Agreed. We all know that. But let me tell you something. About your mom's side of the family, I don't know much." He shot Mom a look weighty with meaning, and she glanced away, pursing her lips.

"We don't know much about them. It's a pity, but that's another story. On this side, you come from people uprooted from their homes by bigots and murderers. From Romania to Winnipeg, let me tell you something, that's no holiday trip. But when they came here, may God bless this country, they could start over. And they did. They didn't give up. Okay, they didn't get rich or run for office, but they made a place to stand on."

He was trying to make me feel bad, like I was letting down the whole Lazarovitch clan, whose name became Lane when they came to Canada.

"This is all just Jewish guilt!" I said angrily.

Grandma's eyes lit up, her hand darted to cover her mouth, and she laughed. Grandpa pointed at me as a cloud of anger crossed his features. Then he laughed too, throwing his head back and letting go.

"What a smart alec," he said.

"Zack, it's done," Mom said, her brows set in a firm line, her dark eyes fiery. "Live with it, or don't. But if you mess up, don't look around for someone to blame."

On the way back to our new house, crammed together with my two silent parents in that loser pickup, I looked out the windows as the buildings and expressways gave way to farmland and fence rows, knowing nothing would change.

In what she thought of as her no-nonsense voice Ms. Song told me to stay after class. "Time for a reality check, Zack," she added.

It was a few days after the incident at Elora Gorge Park, and our history class had spent the whole period taking a test on seventeenth-century British North America, not exactly a captivating topic. To say I had failed the test badly would be putting it mildly—which didn't help my already rotten average. I could just imagine the sermon Song was about to deliver.

Even though I was failing her subject, I liked her. Always in a hurry and often late, she was a tightly wrapped bundle of pure energy who flew up and down the halls like a demented sparrow. Bits of yarn held her long, crow black hair behind her neck; her multicolored dresses hung on her like curtains, almost brushing her clunky discount-store running shoes. Not what you'd call a fashion model. But she knew so much history that her students called her The Book.

"Come up here," she commanded in a not very commanding voice after the last kid had left the room and closed the door.

I stood by her desk, trying hard to work a look of remorse into my face. I knew what was coming.

"What are you trying to do, Zack, convince me that you're a dope?"

"No."

"Can you explain your mark?"

"I didn't study too much, I guess."

"You didn't study," she scoffed. "Listen, my cat could have passed this test. It was all content, memory work. You didn't have to stretch your brain one little bit."

She paused, waiting for me to say something. I didn't.

"So what's the problem? You don't like history, is that it?"

Never tell a teacher you don't like her subject. "It's okay, I guess. I like it all right."

"Ah, so it's me, then."

"No," I answered hastily, this time truthfully.

"You don't like the class?"

"It's okay."

"The ambience doesn't suit you? Your desk is too small? Come on, Zack, give me a clue here, will you?"

"I don't know. It's hard to explain."

That was true too. I wanted to get away from that Mickey-Mouse town so much that my teeth ached, and my only way out was a college or university. To be accepted at those places I needed a diploma, with a decent average. Which meant studying hard and doing assignments diligently and handing them in on time. I knew all that.

But I just couldn't get down to work. Every night I'd

climb dutifully up to my room after supper, full of determination, sit at my desk, open my books and . . . nothing. All my resolve would fade. I'd have a million excuses, a thousand diversions. I would doodle, get up and fiddle with the radio settings, sharpen pencils even though I always used a pen, go out for a run, watch TV, promising myself after just one show I'd get at the books.

What was wrong? It wasn't as if I had an active social life. It wasn't as if I had *any* social life. Teams and school clubs? I belonged to none. I had no girlfriend, no car, no job, no pets—not even a goldfish. Nothing stood between me and my studies. So why couldn't I concentrate? Why couldn't I get even a little bit interested in Shakespeare or chemical reactions or, heaven help me, British North America?

The Book broke in on my thoughts. "Zack, I'll make a deal with you. Maybe you can salvage this credit. It's a one-time offer, take it or leave it. Interested?"

No, I wanted to say. An impending earthquake couldn't raise my interest these days.

"Yes, Ms. Song."

Her brows creased a little. "Hmm. Do try to contain your enthusiasm. Okay, the responsibility to pass history, as I never tire of reminding you people, rests entirely on your shoulders. I'm offering you a chance to do an independent study project. Your task is to come up with a research topic, your own choice. The only stipulation is that it has to be something to do with local history. Bring your idea to me within, oh, three days. If I approve it, you use our class time to work on your own project. And if you do a decent job on it, you'll get your credit. What do you say? Agreed?"

I knew she was throwing me a lifeline. Based on my results so far and the time left in the semester, there was almost no chance that I'd pass history.

"Agreed."

She began to gather up her books and stuff them into an already bulging briefcase. "Okay. See you tomorrow."

On the way out I paused at the door. "Ms. Song?"

"Yes, Zack."

"Thanks."

Local history, I mused as I walked across the parking lot to the bus. Around me, kids swarmed, shrieking good-byes as they headed for their buses. Of all the restrictions Song could have put on me, it had to be that. She offered me a way out, then made it as difficult as possible for me. What could have happened around this tedious town? How could I possibly find anything to research? Maybe Dad could help. He had a whole university library available to him.

"Zack! Zack, wait up!"

Jen's voice chased me across the parking lot, causing heads to turn in my direction. I hadn't seen her for a couple of days, but she had been in homeroom that morning, glancing my way a few times, probably looking for a chance to take a shot at me.

Part of the reason why I had been so surprised by

Jen's reaction to her cousin's remark that day in the park was that, up until then, she had been friendly and helpful, showing me the ropes. I had even thought of asking her out. But I had seen her kind before. Though not openly hostile themselves, they would stand by and listen or watch while someone trashed a kid because they didn't have the guts to object. Or they were hearing what they'd like to have said themselves. Teachers referred to it as peer pressure. I called it cowardice.

I ignored her call and reached for the stair railing of the bus. A hand clutched my shoulder from behind.

"Zack!"

I shook her off.

"Zack, I need to talk to you."

"You going in or not?" a mouthy grade-niner asked, pushing past me up the steps.

I turned to face Jen. Her face was flushed and she was breathing hard.

"What do you want?" I asked.

Her eyes flicked from side to side, conscious that we stood in the middle of a throng. Behind me, the bus engine rumbled and kids yelled back and forth, opened and closed windows.

Jen took a breath. When she spoke, her voice trembled a little and she hurried her words, as if making a prepared speech.

"Zack, I, um, I want to apologize for my cousin. She's a real jerk. I don't even like her. She was visiting with her parents and I got stuck with her all afternoon. I'm sorry about what she said."

"You laughed, Jen. You thought it was funny. So did Dave."

"I didn't think it was funny at all. I thought it was awful. I was so shocked and then embarrassed that I laughed. I didn't know what to say. But after you left, I told her what I thought of her and her crappy attitude."

She raked her hair away from her face with her fingers. "Zack, I just want you to know I'm not her."

"That's nice," I said, hearing the hard edge in my voice.

She looked down at her loafers, which were speckled with mud. "I thought you and I were friends," she mumbled.

"Yeah, well, so did I," I said, and turned to climb aboard the bus.

When I got home and pushed open the front door with more force than was necessary, slamming it behind me, I heard the blues floating from Mom's studio. She was working up a new song—I didn't recognize the tune. I dropped my books on the table by the door, kicked off my high-tops, and went to tell her I was home. When she was composing, a nuclear bomb could go off in the next room and she'd never notice.

Mom had spent a lot of money soundproofing the room and installing recording equipment so she could do most of her work at home rather than rent a professional sound studio. The thick, insulated door was open, so I knew she was rehearsing, not recording. Like my father, she didn't like to be disturbed when she was working, so I stuck my head around the corner and waved. Fingers skittering from fret to fret as the notes wove themselves into patterns, Mom smiled, nodded, causing her earrings to sway, and closed her eyes. Too bad, I thought, I hadn't inherited her powers of concentration along with her nose.

As I turned to leave, the guitar broke into a traditional blues chord progression.

"Now here's the handsome stranger," she sang, calling up her best Chicago street sound.

Coming home to see his ma,
His momma says, 'Hey, son of mine,
It's time to mow the lawn.'

Ah, hell, I thought, then laughed, despite my sour mood. I walked into the room and picked up one of the guitars that sat like a waiting butler in a stand. Copying her chord pattern and attempting to mimic her accent, I sang right back at her.

'Oh,' said the handsome stranger,
'I just ain't in the mood,
I'll mow the lawn some other time,
Now, I need solitude.'

A pretty lame rhyme, but the best I could do. I put down the guitar and turned to go.

"She says, 'You may be handsome,'" I heard behind me.

She says, 'You may be strong,
With money and a fancy car.
You still got to mow the lawn.'

And without missing a beat she switched back to the tune she was working on.

Talking my mother out of something was more trouble than pushing a dump truck uphill, so I went to my room, changed into shorts and a T-shirt, and walked to the garage to haul out the ancient gas-powered lawn mower.

That's another thing I hate about this damn country-style living, I thought as I pushed the rackety mower back and forth. In the city a lawn is a sensible size; here it's like mowing a farm.

By the time I had assassinated the last blade of grass in the backyard, careful not to yield to temptation and accidentally mow down Mom's new lilac shrubs, Dad was home. He was lifting his briefcase out of the truck, his cardigan draped over it, when I shoved the mower into the garage.

"Hey, Farmer Zack," he said. "How's things on the back forty?"

I had no idea what he meant by the "back forty" and no intention of asking.

"Hi, Dad. Mom's making me do slave labor again," I said grumpily.

Dad looked at the uneven stripes on the front lawn and the tufts of grass I had missed in my careless swipes to and fro. "Well, you got most of it," he said.

"You should be grateful. I'm the son of a musician and an academic. You're lucky I didn't run over my feet."

"Right," he said. "Good point."

I followed him into the house and headed for the shower.

My lawn mower martyrdom did not exempt me from clean-up detail after dinner—my parents refused to buy a dishwasher. I was putting the last plate in the cupboard when the doorbell rang. A moment later Mom came into the kitchen.

"Someone's here for you," she said with a grin from ear to ear. "Where have you been keeping her?"

"Keeping who?"

"Oh, I see. It's a secret thing, is it?" she said, and walked into the studio.

Standing inside our front door, wearing a school sweatshirt and baggy warm-up shorts, was Jen. Her hair was pulled back from her face, held in place with two gold barrettes. I could smell her floral perfume across the room.

"I didn't like the way we left things," she began while I was trying to think of something to say.

Neither had I. While I was mowing the lawn I had replayed our conversation a dozen times. Had I been too hard on her, refusing her apology like that?

As if in answer she took a step toward me, moving in close, and before I could speak she threw her arms around my neck and kissed me.

Since I had met Jen I had wondered how her lips would feel, and now I knew. They were even softer than I had imagined or hoped, and the firm press of her breasts against my chest put all thoughts of anger out of my mind. Sometime during the long kiss I put my arms around her and pulled her closer, tasting the minty flavor of her mouth, breathing in the fragrance of her hair.

"I've wanted to do that for a long time," she said,

breaking the kiss but not the tight hold of her arms.

"Me too," I croaked. "Maybe we should do it again."

Jen flushed as she looked behind me. Dad was passing through toward the kitchen, an empty mug in his hand.

"Don't mind me," he said in his playful voice. "I didn't see anything. I'm not even here." And he disappeared.

"Great timing, Dad," I muttered.

Jen laughed. "Well, I guess I'll be going. I just wanted to—"

"Can't you stay?"

"I'm running an errand for my mother. She'll wonder. You mean a lot to me, Zack. I wanted you to know."

"Y'all done kissed a nigra," I drawled. "What would y'all's cousin think?"

"If she knew what she was missing, she'd be jealous. Well, bye. Call me later if you want."

"Okay."

I walked her to her car and stood in the driveway, happily confused, as she drove away, then went back into the house.

"Can I come out now?"

"Knock it off, Dad," I said, taking a can of tonic water from the fridge.

He was standing at the window, looking out over the yard. "Come here. Look at the way the light is falling on the river."

I stood behind him. The slanting light made the water look like a strip of pewter and lit up Mom's little lilac bushes and the flower garden she had put in beside them.

"Hey, I think I've got an idea," I blurted.

"An idea about what?"

"Oh, nothing," I said, and I sprinted up the stairs.

3 1112 01205 0411

I closed my bedroom door tightly, switched on the light on my desk, and got down on my hands and knees. I grasped a corner of the plastic bag and dragged it out from under the bed, lifted it onto the desk, and removed the box. The box gave off a damp odor of earth and decay. Inside, the iron Cs clanked. I sat at the desk and examined my accidental discovery.

Maybe, just maybe, the thing might yield something interesting and important, and if it did I would make meticulous notes and drawings and dazzle The Book into giving me a history credit.

Rummaging around in my desk, I collected a few pencils (already sharpened during wasted hours), a small ruler, a notebook, and a magnifying glass I hadn't touched since I was a kid. On hot summer days I had used it to burn my initials into baseball bats, fences, and plastic toys, and to incinerate unlucky ants as they marched across the parking lot of our apartment building. I then slipped the box back into the bag, added my tools, and crept downstairs and out the back door to the garage.

There was a workbench there, unused since we had moved in, with a fluorescent light above it and all sorts of tools, cleaning solvents, rags, and paintbrushes at hand. It took a few minutes to clear a work space.

I placed the box in the center of the bench and tossed the bag away, then took out the objects and put them aside, replacing the lid. With a small paintbrush I whisked away the dirt encrusted on the surface of the box—not so difficult now that the soil had dried—to find that the wood was covered with some kind of material. Paper? Cloth? No, leather. Then I wiped the surface clean with a damp rag, working slowly because the leather wanted to crumble and flake. When the outside of the box was clean I brushed out the moldy inside.

The box was about fourteen inches long and half as wide. The front panel held a brass lock with the hasp missing. Two brass hinges had broken away from the back panel but were still attached to the lid. In the center of the lid was a small, curved brass handle, barely big enough to get three fingers under it. A fancy gold border ran around the lid's edge.

I used my magnifying glass, feeling like a Sherlock Holmes wannabe, to examine the border, and that was when I noticed a diamond with the same design around the handle. And there was something else. I peered at the surface, my face inches from the musty-smelling leather, like a miser looking for a lost penny.

A lot of the gold—or whatever it was—had flaked off, but I was pretty sure I could make out an ornate letter, *G*, then a shape I couldn't identify, then an *R*. It took more squinting and guessing before I knew that the shape between the letters had been a representation of a crown.

With a growing sense of excitement, I put down the glass, rubbed my eyes, stretched the stiffness out of my back and neck, and began to make notes, describing the box in detail. I used the ruler to draw it to scale. Then, in my clumsy, unartistic style, I attempted to copy the design of the border. Last, using the glass again to double check, I drew the crown.

"Zack, where are you?" my mother called.

I dropped my pencil and scooted out of the garage. "I'm out here, Mom. Be in in a minute."

"What are you doing?"

"Nothing, just a school project."

"In the *garage*?"

"Be in soon," I repeated.

When I heard the door shut I let out my breath and stepped back into the garage. Why didn't I tell her what I was up to? Why did I want to keep the box and its contents a secret, at least for the time being? Because if things didn't work out I didn't want to look like a loser. I was a little embarrassed, getting excited about my discovery. If I had been seven years old it would have been okay. It would have been nifty. Gee, golly, I could say, this sure is peachy. But not now. I was sensitive about looking like an idiot. Sue me.

I set the box aside and brushed the dirt from the top of the bench. Then I picked up the bit of skin that had held the metal nugget. The remnants of the little bag were now dry and stiff and would snap like a potato chip if I wasn't careful. I poured an inch of solvent into an empty peanut tin and dropped the nugget in, swirling it around. Then, using a small brush, I cleaned it. The solvent quickly dissolved the grime from the surface of the metal, which, when polished with a dry rag, gave off a bronze glow. It was an almost perfect sphere with a rough surface.

I examined it with my Sherlock Holmes ant-burner, my pulse quickening. When I had dug it up I had wondered for a split second, could it be gold? And if it was, how much was it worth?

I packed up my loot and crept into the house by the back door. After stopping in the kitchen for a small sealable freezer bag, I silently climbed up to my room. I wrapped the box in an old T-shirt and slid it under the bed, then put the nugget into the plastic bag and buried it in my top drawer under my socks and underwear. That done, I undressed and hopped into bed. Even if this little investigation of mine fell flat, even if I ended up looking like a fool, maybe I'd be able to salvage something from the whole exercise.

That day had started out even worse than most. The faint hope I had been given by The Book had evaporated when Jen had spoken to me in the parking lot, reawakening a long familiar humiliation and anger. Now, after Jen's visit and my work in the garage, it seemed that the spring might not be so bad after all.

But thoughts about Jen, about school, and The Book's offer marched around in my brain, keeping sleep away. I got out of bed, shrugged into my bathrobe, and went downstairs to drug myself with a little TV watching.

I wasn't surprised to see that a light was on in Dad's

study. He had always been a night owl, preferring to work when the house was quiet, and a few days earlier I had heard him tell Mom he was under the gun to meet a deadline. Some article or other for one of the periodicals he contributed to.

He had changed into striped pajamas and what he called his Balzac, a roomy woolen robe with a hood, and he sat behind his desk, reading glasses perched on the end of his aquiline nose. A hockey player throughout his childhood and teens, he was solidly built without looking lumpy like many ex-athletes. His black hair had a natural curl that made him look young.

His desk lamp, the only illumination in the room, threw a wide pool of light over the books and papers scattered across his desk in typical disorderly order, and cast a yellow glow on his face as he read. He was running thick fingers across his broad chin the way he always did when concentrating.

As I stepped into the room my eye was drawn to the picture of the neo-Nazi with the military cap outside the courthouse, only now he was upside down. Dad had printed out the stuff I had found for him on the Internet and the sheets were lined up along the edge of the desk.

"Oh, hi, Zack," he said, looking up. "Bedbugs getting to you?"

"Yeah. Can't sleep. Is that stuff any use?"

"Definitely. Not much that's new or original, but I can cite some of it in the monograph I'm working on."

"That's good."

"But I think next time it might be better if you just give me the Web site address. Don't bother downloading."

"Sure."

"We don't want the inestimable Ms. O'Neil on our case again," he added, smiling.

We were silent for a moment. I pointed to the printouts.

"I guess it never ends, does it, Dad?"

He lowered the page and removed his glasses, then linked his fingers to form one thick fist on top of the page. "No." He lifted his chin toward the photo of Krupp. "Not as long as there are pathetic misfits like him around. And not as long as societies produce unhappy and hateful people to follow them."

"Dad, are you sorry sometimes that you're a Jew?"

He sat back in his old leather wing chair and disappeared into the shadows. Then he leaned forward and the light crossed his face again to reveal a frown. He looked into my face, as if examining me.

"When I was growing up, my religion, my culture, didn't mean much to me. Your grandma and grandpa pushed it pretty hard, and I guess that's why. It's very important to them, but I've always believed a person has to come to these things on his own. So I've always been pretty secular."

He paused and looked at his wall of books. "But sorry? No. Never."

"So, does reading crap like that . . . does it make you mad? No, that's not what I mean. Do you take it personally?"

"Has something happened, Zack?"

"No, no," I lied. "I was just wondering."

His left eyebrow rose slightly—an involuntary reaction he hardly noticed most of the time that told me he didn't buy my answer. But he let it go.

"No, I don't take it personally—well, that's not entirely true. I try not to, and most of the time I succeed. But it's hard. Isn't it?"

"Yeah."

A tone I couldn't identify came into his voice when he began to speak again.

"Zack, over the long span of history the Jews have been ghettoized and/or run out of every country in Europe. After the Holocaust they made their own country, and since then people have been trying to kick them out of there too. But the Jews are still around. And do you know why?"

Without waiting for an answer he continued, punctuating his thoughts by tapping his index finger on the desktop. "Because, when things get bad, the Jews don't sit around in bars" *tap* "or loiter on street corners" *tap* "moaning and complaining about being oppressed." *tap* "First, we build a synagogue." *tap* "Then we build a school." *tap* "Then we start over." He stopped, as if surprised at his own feelings. "Sorry, didn't mean to make a speech."

"Dad?"

"Uh-huh?"

"You said 'we.'"

He laughed. "I guess I did, at that."

Back in my bed, I lay on my back, studying the

pattern made on the ceiling by the moon that hung in the sky above the river behind the house. I wondered, when a guy like Krupp looks at me, does he hate me half as much because I'm only half-Jewish, or twice as much because I'm half-black, too?

Then I remembered something Mom had told me when I was little—young enough to sit on her lap. She had taken me to a park near our apartment building and I had been playing with a few other kids on the climbers and in the sandbox, and when she called to me that it was time to go home, when she was brushing dust from my clothes and poking sand from the spaces between the laces on my running shoes with her long fingers, I asked her why the other kids didn't have black and white parents.

Holding me tightly on her knee, Mom had pointed to a giant oak on the edge of the play area. "You're like that tree," she told me. "You have two strong roots going way down into the ground, strong enough to hold you up no matter how hard the wind blows."

I hadn't understood her, and I soon lost interest in my question because an ice-cream truck happened by. But I had thought about her metaphor a few times since then, and as I lay in bed after talking to Dad, I felt I grasped it. I did have two roots. One I knew a lot about; I had grown up with my grandma and grandpa at the center of my life. But I had been cut off from the other root, and for some reason the older I got the more I resented Mom for doing that to me.

As soon as the big yellow monster let me out at the end of our drive I jogged to the house to get the nugget, shining and inviting inside the clear plastic bag, and jammed it deep into the pocket of my jeans.

Mom wasn't in her studio, so I knew she'd be outside. Sure enough, I heard her humming as soon as I pushed open the back door. She was on her knees in the middle of a patch of newly turned earth, a trowel in one gloved hand, some kind of pink flower in the other, and a sheen of sweat on her face. Around her, empty flats were scattered in the late afternoon sun.

"Hi, Mom. I'm on my way downtown to see Jen at work," I said, letting the door slam behind me and heading for the garage.

"Wait a minute. I want you to—"

"Later," I called, pretending I hadn't heard her.

I unlocked my one valuable possession—my mountain bike, a birthday present from my grandparents the year before. ("It's too expensive," Dad had said to Grandma. "You're spoiling him," Mom had added. "Where's the key?" I had asked.) I strapped on my helmet, pushed the bike out of the garage and hopped on.

The Fergus Market, at Queen and St. David on the

bank of the river, was once some kind of factory or mill that had used the river for power. Like a lot of the buildings in Fergus it was constructed of quarried stone. Now it was a sort of semi-upscale mall, with the Chamber of Commerce, a couple of shops that sold overpriced clothing from Scotland, and a farmer's market. I got off my bike, removed the seat and front wheel, and locked them and the bike to a stand.

I stood in the doorway blinking while my eyes adjusted to the semi-gloom, then headed for the fast-food stand where Jen worked after school and on weekends. The Market Grill was in the central aisle, flanked on one side by the Heritage Clothing shop, which, according to the sign, sold "only organic apparel"—which was what, I wondered, shirts made of cornstalks? pants woven from hay?—and on the other by an antique stand displaying a lot of old coal-oil lamps and broken chairs.

Jen was serving up a paper plate stacked high with a cheeseburger and fries to a man in a sweat suit who looked like he'd be better off with a double order of diet pills. She took his money and put it in the register.

"Hi," I said. "Got any food here?"

She smiled. She had on a navy blue T-shirt with "Market Grill" on the front in white, the letters following her curves, and her thick hair was pulled back and tied with a white scarf, accentuating her large eyes and oval face.

"Buddy, if you want *food* you came to the wrong place."

"Do you have a break coming up soon?"

"Not really, Zack. I just got here twenty minutes ago. There's only me and the boss. He's a slave driver."

"Okay. Um, I've got an errand to run, then I'll come back."

"Good. Come here." She waggled her finger, as if she wanted to whisper in my ear. But she kissed me instead. "Think that'll hold you?"

"Maybe," I said, and I left the market.

I climbed up the short hill to St. Andrew, turned left, and walked past the library to Piffard's Custom Jewelry—a word some people in Fergus pronounced *joolery*—a small store squeezed between a real-estate broker and the Theatre on the Grand.

A bell tinkled above my head as I pushed open the door, rehearsing what I was going to say. A glass case ran the length of the store to my right, containing costume jewelry, watches, and fancy china cups. A man with a very large hooked nose and a very bushy walrus mustache stood at the back of the shop behind another glass case, writing something in a notebook. The stub of an unlit cigar was clamped in the corner of his mouth. He had a tiny magnifying glass on a stem clipped to the wire frame of his glasses. At his back was a curtained doorway.

He looked up. "Help you, son?" he asked in a voice that suggested he'd just as soon wash the floor.

I approached the counter. "I hope so," I said, fishing the plastic bag from my pocket. "I was wondering, could you tell me what this is made of?" I shook the nugget onto the red velvet pad on top of the case.

The man put down his pen and pushed the

notebook aside. He picked up the nugget and held it to the light between thumb and forefinger.

"Interesting," he said, the cigar bobbing. "What is it?"

"I don't know."

He pulled a lamp with a circular fluorescent bulb toward him and switched it on. In the center of the bulb was a magnifying glass. He held the nugget under the lamp, turning it around several times with fingers made huge by the glass.

"Where did you get it?"

"It's been in the family a long time," I said, feeling justified in my lie because of his prying. "I inherited it. From my grandfather. I think—That is, I was told it's gold and I thought maybe a professional jeweler could tell me for sure."

"It was cast," he said, continuing his examination, "but not expertly. And not properly. That's why it's a little rough." He adjusted the little lens in front of one side of his glasses and squinted at the nugget some more.

"And it contains impurities."

His voice had been warming all along. He was clearly interested in the nugget.

"Bit of a mystery, isn't it?" he said, switching off the lamp. He smiled for the first time and the cigar tilted toward the ceiling.

"Sure is," I said lamely.

"This'll take a few minutes."

"Okay."

He locked the jewelry case, pushed the curtain aside

and disappeared. No one came into the shop as I waited with rising suspense. After what seemed like half an hour but was ten minutes by my watch, he came back into the shop. A thin blue line of smoke rose from the cigar. When he dropped the nugget on the red velvet I saw that he had scraped a thin line on it.

"Yup, interesting," he repeated. "I think it's shot."

"You mean ruined?"

He laughed. With one eye squinted almost shut against the cigar smoke, he said, "No, no. Shot. Rifle shot. A bullet. You were right, it must be very old. Strange thing for an heirloom, though."

"Yeah, it's been sort of a family mystery for years. So, is it gold?"

"It's gold, all right. Not high grade, though. Maybe ten carat, and like I said, it's full of impurities."

"How much is it worth?"

"Oh, I could give you, maybe, a few hundred for it."

"You'd buy it from me?"

"I make custom jewelry from time to time for certain clients. I could use it. But like I said. It's not very high grade. And I'd have to see a letter from your parents giving you permission to sell it."

I slipped the nugget back into the baggie.

"No problem," I said. "Thanks a lot."

Practically bursting with happiness at my sudden wealth, I rushed back to the market and Jen asked her boss if she could take a fifteen-minute break. She drew two giant colas from the machine when the boss wasn't looking and we walked around the displays, holding hands and pretending to be interested in the merchandise. I fought with myself. One minute I'd be on the verge of telling her about the nugget, the next I'd be counseling myself to keep it secret a while longer, at least until I talked to The Book about my research project.

"Why not come over tonight and we'll watch a movie," Jen said as we returned to the grill.

"Um, maybe not."

"Why? Got another date?" she said playfully.

"No, it's . . . well, would your parents be okay with me visiting?"

"What do you mean?"

"I mean, do they know about me?"

"Sure. I told them I'm going out with you."

We stopped. Jen went behind the counter and put on her apron.

"I mean, do they *know* about me?"

Jen looked at me curiously, then her brows creased in anger. "That's kind of insulting, you know, Zack."

I didn't respond. I tossed my empty cup into the garbage can beside the counter.

"Maybe," she said stiffly, "you're a little too sensitive about that."

"Maybe that's easy for you to say."

"My parents are color blind, Zack. Okay?"

"Okay. Sorry."

"Come over around seven." Then, turning to her work, she added, "If you feel like it."

I left the market, depressed by the knowledge that,

although things were going good between us, deep down I still wondered about her.

Before supper was put on the table—Dad was cooking up one of his culinary monstrosities, macaroni with cheese and ham—I helped Mom in the garden, breaking up lumps of soil with a hoe, working up a good sweat. After we had struggled through the meal, making fun of the "yellow death," as Mom had named the dish, I hurried through my kitchen chores and drove over to Jen's. She lived in a small stone house near St. Joseph's Church.

Her parents were very nice. They said hello and cleared out of the family room as if on cue, then Jen and I watched a horror flick. The atmosphere was a little frosty at first—in the room, not the movie—but after we had made a few jokes about the number one vampire, who was about as scary as a wet rag, we were laughing. About halfway through the movie Jen climbed onto my lap. I don't know what happened after that—in the movie, not the room.

I got home about ten thirty, checked in with my parents, who were playing Scrabble at the kitchen table and arguing good-naturedly about a word Mom said Dad had just made up out of thin air, and took my loot from under the bed.

The two rolled-up straps were even stiffer and harder, because they had dried out, and when I attempted once more to unroll them they resisted. The ends were folded back and sewn to form loops. Probably, I thought, they were belts of some kind, and the loops had held buckles. If they were, whoever owned them must have been as fat as a tub because, if stretched out, they would have been pretty long.

So I made notes on them, and sketched them in my normal incompetent way, and set them aside. The Cs of iron were even less interesting. I took them to the garage and dropped them into a pail of solvent and went back into the house to wash the rust from my hands. Once more I began to doubt that the stuff I had found would make a project solid enough to satisfy Ms. Song. But I had no other ideas.

The Book rushed into the library, a thick sheaf of papers in one hand, a cup of coffee in the other, her running shoes chirping on the tile floor. She sat down beside me at a table in a quiet corner of the reading room and plunked down her cup, slopping coffee on the Formica top.

"Shoot!" she exclaimed, wiping up the puddle with a tissue, her idea of a really raunchy curse, I guessed. "Okay, Zack, I'm all ears. What do you have?"

I had ridden the bus to school with my treasures on my knee in a gym bag, my stomach fluttering, alternating between hope and the certainty that I was about to make a monumental fool of myself. "What *is* this junk?" I imagined The Book sneering. "I gave you a break and you come to me with something you dug up in your *yard*?"

If she doesn't accept my proposal, my history credit goes down the drain and I might as well quit school now and avoid the June rush, I had thought as I sat fidgeting in the library, waiting for her to be late.

My notes were carefully arranged before me on the table, along with the kindergarten-level drawings. My gym bag was on the floor beside me.

"Well," I began, "you'll probably think this is a terminally goofy idea—"

"Nice sales pitch," she interrupted, and sipped her coffee.

Great, I thought, she's laughing at me already. But I plowed forward. I related how I had found the box, dug it up, cleaned and inspected both it and its contents. As I spoke I showed her my notes, pointed to the sketches, drew the objects one by one from the bag for dramatic effect.

As I spoke my confidence grew. She sat still and silent, her coffee cooling beside her, her hands resting on the pile of tests, fingers interlocked. I ended by handing her the iron Cs, now scraped clean of rust.

"And I have no idea what these metal things are," I concluded. "But my proposal is, I want to find out what all this stuff is and how it ended up buried in the ground behind our house."

"You really don't know what this is?" she asked, taking the Cs from me. Her voice was quiet. "Are you serious?"

Damn. I had lost her. She hadn't been interested at all; she had been letting me say my piece, politely, because that was the kind of teacher she was. Now would come the gentle criticism, the soft-spoken rejection.

"Yes, Ms. Song. I don't have a clue."

"I do."

"And?" As if I cared at this point.

"Well, you'll have to find out. I'm not telling. But, Zack, prepare yourself. You're not going to like it."

"You mean you accept the project?"

"Are you kidding? I think it sounds great. And you've made a terrific start, with your notes and all. Come on, I'll give you some stuff to get you started."

When we left the library, I was juggling my gym bag and six huge books Song had pulled from the shelves and slapped into my hands as I hurried behind her through the stacks.

"See you tomorrow, Zack. I'm late. Happy hunting." And with that she tore off down the hall.

I stumbled to my locker and stored all the stuff, then began gathering my books for my next class.

What had she meant when she'd said I should prepare myself?

The books Song had given me were about the American Revolutionary War, the War of 1812, and local history. I would have bet Fergus had about enough history to fill a pamphlet, but there were two fat volumes.

That evening I sat at my now crowded desk with a can of tonic water and a bowl of taco chips, Miles Davis on the stereo, and set to work. I liked the *Illustrated Encyclopedia of the American Revolution* best because it was all pictures. I flipped through it at random, wondering what The Book thought I'd find in there, since my box had been dug up in Canada. There were page after page of muskets, powder horns, uniforms, belts, swords, hats; pioneer tools like axes—I recognized the ax head I had found in the yard—adzes, plows, and harnesses; dresses, bonnets, breeches, and shoes. Three CDs were consumed as I pored over the photos, and by the time I closed the book I was able to make four lengthy additions to my notes. And I had generated lots of questions.

The soot-covered stones I had dug up from the same hole as the box had probably been remnants of a pioneer cabin's chimney and fireplace. Which meant that our house was built almost on top of the site. Who had lived on our land? Had the cabin burned down or rotted away after being abandoned?

Piffard the jeweler had probably been right: The nugget seemed to have been cast in a bullet mold. There were pictures of these tools in the book. But why cast gold as a bullet? To shoot a werewolf? I wondered, laughing and spraying corn-chip dust all over my work. Was it easier to carry or hide the gold as shot rather than dust? Or had it been a coin, melted down?

The leather straps, I deduced, were exactly that, not belts. In the book was a picture of a Butler's Rangers dress uniform. The rangers were a corps of British soldiers who had fought the Americans guerrilla-style, with Indian allies. The straps were worn crisscrossed over the shoulders and chest and held a sword on one side and an ammunition box on the other. Had the cabin owner, the pioneer, once been an army man?

That question seemed to be answered by the identity of the box—and that was the most exciting discovery. It was called a document box—I saw it looking at me from page 256 of the book. The crown represented England and the initials *G R* stood for Georgius Rex—

King George, who reigned during the time of the American Revolution.

In other words, my silly half-rotten box was more than two hundred years old! And that proved that the contents were at least as old.

That night sleep came late. My mind spun, throwing out question after question. Who had lived on our land on the banks of the Grand River two hundred years ago? Why had he or she buried the box? To hide it? To save it from or for someone?

"The thing to do," I whispered into the darkness, "is search the title to the land." I had learned when Mom and Dad bought the place that a lawyer had to do a "title search" first to make sure there were no financial liens on the property, and to be certain the person selling it actually owned it. Dad had explained that the registry office could tell you all the proprietors of a piece of land since the Crown had granted it to its first owner.

Maybe if I did that I'd find a clue to the person who buried the box, the nugget, the straps and—

It was then I remembered the iron Cs. What the hell, I thought, I can't sleep anyway.

I stood at the kitchen sink, having used up most of a box of steel-wool pot cleaners, up to my elbows in dirty soapy water, working quietly so as not to wake up my parents. The solvent I had soaked the iron in had loosened most of the surface rust, which came off fairly easily with the steel wool. After half an hour's scrubbing I decided that the thing was as clean as it was going to get. I dried the Cs with a dish towel—leaving it stained with rust—and returned with the iron to my room.

Under my desk lamp the ring was blackish, its surface pitted and scarred from corrosion. As I ran my fingers, now tender from the scrubbing, along it I noticed a place where the roundness had been ground flat.

I trained my magnifying glass on the spot. Barely visible were three letters scraped or punched into the metal. *R P*, then a big space, then a *T*. Once more a rummage in the desk drawer. Congratulating myself that I never threw anything away, I opened the smallest blade of the Swiss Army knife Mom had given me when I was ten. Carefully, I scraped the metal between the letters. Slowly, one by one, the rest of them emerged: *R. PIERPOINT.*

My enthusiasm soared. I had a name. I had a place to start.

The Wellington County Museum, a great gray pile of local quarried stone shaped like a shoe box lying on the long end, with a central tower, sat brooding on the top of a big hill on City Road 18 between Fergus and Elora, as uninviting as a prison. In fact, it used to be one—of a sort. According to the plaque bolted to the wall at the entrance, it was built in 1877 as "the House of Industry and Refuge"—in other words, a poorhouse.

I locked up my bike and shouldered my backpack. Just inside the door was a staircase to the left and beside it a small counter of polished wood. Behind the counter an elderly woman sat at a cluttered desk, a book open in front of her. She turned as she heard the door hiss shut behind me.

"Hello," she said. "Is this your first visit to our museum?" Her hair was silvery white, her face wrinkled and kindly.

"Yes, it is."

"Well, the fee is four dollars. Two for students."

"I was wondering, is there someone who I can talk to, who knows history and stuff?"

Way to go, Zack, I thought. History and stuff. In a museum. What a moron.

"You mean the curator?"

"Sure, that's right."

"Just a moment, please." She lifted the phone, pressed a button, and spoke softly for a moment. "He'll be right out."

"Thanks."

For some reason I had expected that everyone who worked in a museum would be old, but the guy who came through the door behind the staircase was in his thirties, with a rangy build and a shock of vivid red hair. He wore a denim shirt and cork sandals.

"Can I help you?" he greeted me.

"I'm doing a school project and I wondered if you would look at something for me."

"Come this way."

He led me into a small office whose walls were lined with shelves holding books, knickknacks, boxes of computer diskettes and various artifacts. On the file-strewn desk were a phone, three coffee mugs, all of them dirty, a computer, and an elaborate pen set covered with dust.

The curator held out his hand. "I'm Murray Knox."

"Zack Lane." I shook hands with him.

"Take a seat," he invited, lowering himself into a chair behind the desk. "So what's this assignment you're working on?"

I sketched in the background, leaving out a lot, still intent on keeping as much secret as I could. I left out the part about the box, straps, and nugget.

"Well, local history. That's our specialty around here."

I unzipped my pack, lifted out the linked iron Cs and placed them on his desk blotter.

"My, my," he said without touching it, but plainly interested. "You dug that up in your yard?"

"Yes."

"Where do you live?"

I told him.

"Holy cats," he muttered. "Mind if I touch it?"

"No, not at all."

He picked it up and with a deft movement, formed it into a ring with the two box-shaped loops resting against each another. "Uh-huh," he said. He looked up at me, his eyes sparkling with excitement. "What is it you want to know?" he asked me.

"I want to know what it is," I said, recalling The Book's warning that I wouldn't like the answer.

He flushed. "Forgive me," he said. "I didn't realize."

"You didn't realize . . . I don't understand, Mr. Knox."

"It's a neck iron. I take it you've never seen one before?"

"No." A neck iron. Who on earth would wear something like that? And what was this guy's problem, anyway? He was acting as if he'd just told me I had six months to live.

"See here?" He held up the ring, speaking with hesitation. "These D-shaped loops could be held together with a lock and chain. Or, alternatively, if the slave was part of a coffle—a string of slaves—a rope or chain would be passed through and on to the next slave in the line, making escape impossible."

My mind went blank. "Slave?" I whispered, my mouth dry.

"Yes. I'm sorry to embarrass you."

I swallowed hard and straightened up in my chair, only now realizing why he was uneasy. He wasn't the only one.

"There's . . .there's a name on it," I told him.

"Yes, that's not uncommon," he said, hefting the ring in one hand. "That would be the name of the slave's owner—and the slave too, of course."

My head was beginning to return to normal. "I don't understand."

"Normally a slave was given the owner's name. That's the reason, er, blacks in the U.S. and Canada usually have Anglo surnames. Let's see what this says."

He held the ring closer to his face and turned it until he found the letters. "Well, I'll be damned."

"Do you know it?"

"Pierpoint? I surely do. Zack, you've made an important discovery. Come with me."

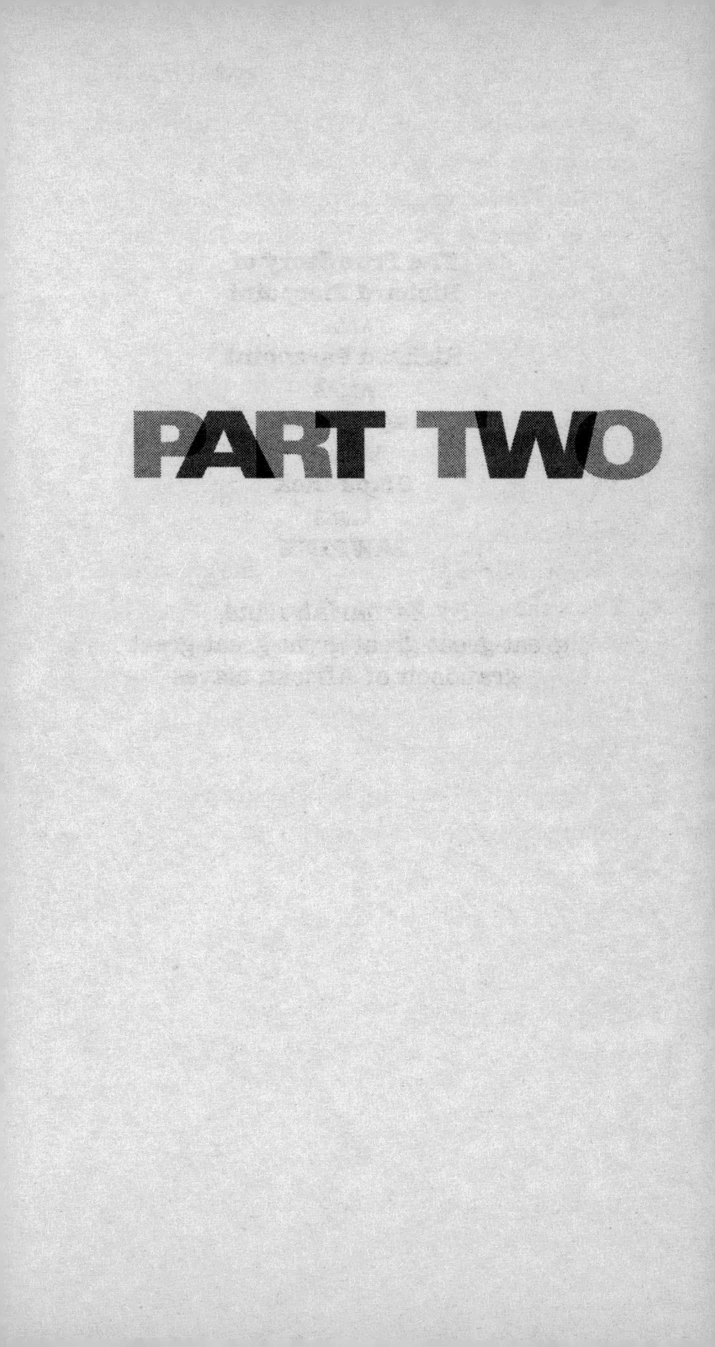

PART TWO

The True Story of
Richard Pierpoint

ALIAS

Richard Parepoint

ALIAS

Captain Dick

ALIAS

Black Dick

ALIAS

PAWPINE

By Zachariah Lane,
great-great-great-great-great-great-grandson of African slaves

Dear Ms. Song,

Here is my project. I'm sorry it's so long, and it's late, long past the due date, but I got very involved in it and I guess I got carried away. I didn't want to leave anything out. I'm not making excuses, but I read two whole books on the "middle passage" alone, not to mention a book on each of the wars. And I spent a zillion hours (well, almost) poring over archival documents at the museum (Mr. Knox was a big help), searching the title to our property at the land registry office, and scanning the Internet for info on a man most people have never heard of.

You have seen the Revolutionary War British document box, the two Butler's Ranger shoulder straps, the nugget, and the slave's neck iron. This project tells the tale of the man who owned them.

I know a history paper is supposed to be objective, but I decided to write this as a story because the facts are only the beginning, and no matter how hard I tried I couldn't stay neutral. I hope I don't fail because of that, but if I do, it's okay.

Thanks for letting me try this. Even if I fail, it was worth it.

P.S. Jen helped me type this. I hope that's legal.

P.P.S. I forgot the footnotes, but it's too late now.

Your student,

Zack

It's as if the events of his life had been written on cards and tossed into the wind. I've gathered the ones I could and tried to arrange them into some kind of order. A lot have been lost. There are many gaps, more questions than answers.

He was born in 1744 in Bondu, Senegambia, West Africa, a river-laced land of steaming marshes and grassy plains. He could have been a Wolof or Mandinke but was probably a Fulani, the dominant tribe of Bondu State. He was likely Moslem and may have known how to read and write. Senegambians grew cotton, tobacco, maize (corn), and rice; they were cunning traders and expert cattle ranchers. To imagine him as an ignorant jungle savage is as logical as suggesting the royal family of England at the time wore smelly animal skins and lived in caves.

Land was plentiful but laborers were not, so war and slavery were bitter facts of life. Tribe raided tribe, carried off the human spoils, and put them to work planting crops or tending cattle. The European slavers who, during the eighteenth century transported 60 percent of West Africa's population across the Atlantic, did not invent slavery. They bought their slaves from Africans.

When he was the age of the average tenth-grade student, he was captured in one of those conflicts. Hands bound behind his back, roped by the neck to other men,

women, and children, he was marc
the broad Gambia River and boated
stream to James Fort, an island fort
near the ocean, and sold to Europeans
Before he was driven aboard the ship that lay at anchor in the estuary, he was grappled to the ground, tallow was smeared on his stomach then covered with oiled paper, and, with an iron heated in a fire until it glowed red, he was branded. He belonged to the Royal African Company. He was cargo.

The "middle passage," the hellish ocean journey to the New World, took anywhere from two weeks to two months, and it's hard to imagine how he survived. He was chained to another man and made to lie hip to hip, shoulder to shoulder on a shelf in the dark, airless, sweltering hold, the next shelf only inches above him. As the ship pitched and rolled under sail, the rough planks ground away his sweat-soaked skin and flesh, leaving open running sores.

The hold was a noxious pit of putrid stench—urine, vomit, excrement, and the sour stink of vinegar used by the slavers in a halfhearted effort to quell the foul odors. Men around him groaned and cried out in the dark in their different languages. Many died, consumed by despair. Each day he was hauled on deck with others, chained to the rail, fed, and forced to dance while sailors tossed buckets of icy seawater on him to wash him down. Some slaves broke free and hurled themselves into the freezing ocean.

Of the many who died, most succumbed to the "bloody flux," chronic dysentery that squeezed the liquid from their bowels in violent, painful spasms and killed them where they lay on the benches drenched in their own reeking waste. On average, the corpses thrown overboard numbered 15 percent of the human cargo.

He refused to die. He fought off the virulent diseases that stalked the ship and the terrible despair that tempted him every minute of every day to give up.

After two months of the horror, a skeleton wrapped tightly in shiny black skin, covered in scabs and sores, his eyes sunken into his head, he was off-loaded, probably in Barbados, given a salve to rub on his ravaged skin, fattened up for a few weeks and, when he looked presentable, taken to auction on the mainland. Where? In the slave market in Charles' Town, South Carolina; in Boston; in New York? Whatever his point of entry into the colonies that "belonged" to Britain, he was bought from the Royal African Company by Pierpoint, a British soldier, and named Richard.

When I started this project I thought that a slave was just a person owned by another person, like a wagon, an ax, or a horse. A slave was someone with no freedom. But what they took from him was more than that. They stole his home, his family, his roots and, maybe worst of all, his name. His religion was called heretical. His language was "mumbo jumbo." His stories and songs were scorned.

There were some things they couldn't take away, though—his willpower and his intelligence, his courage and his dignity.

If the land of Pierpoint's birth was one of slavery, the American colonies in 1760 were, in many ways, worse. There were thousands and thousands of captured Africans laboring on plantations or serving in households. Although they did not remain in bondage for life, there were white slaves too: indentured servants sold to a master for a period of years; convicts transported to the New World and sold as laborers until they had "paid off" the cost of their passage; sailors "pressed" into duty (captured, hauled aboard ship, and not released until the vessel was far out to sea). Owning a human being was an idea that was widely accepted. The man who penned the Declaration of Independence was a plantation owner whose African farmhands were his property, and when he wrote that all men were created equal he meant white males only. The man who wrote "Give me liberty, or give me death" owned more than sixty slaves.

In that land of wagons, horses, dirt roads, huge plantations and primitive isolated farms, frontier towns, and a few cities that were just tiny dots in a vast landscape of unbroken forest, the sixteen-year-old boy from Bondu must always have felt isolated and alone. He was the personal servant of a British officer who probably looked down on most of his own troops, never mind his black slave. Richard Pierpoint had to learn a new language and strange customs. But he did it. He did all that, and more.

And he dropped out of sight for twenty years.

Richard Pierpoint turned up again in, of all places, Fort Niagara, just across the river from present-day Niagara-on-the-Lake. By that time he had earned his freedom by enlisting to fight the Americans for King George, the same king whose chartered slave company had bought, branded, and sold him. He was Captain Dick now, also called Pawpine, a member of Butler's Rangers, which was a part of the British army often supplemented with Indian allies.

What had happened in the twenty years?

The American Revolutionary War, for one thing. It was still raging when Pierpoint arrived in Fort Niagara. At that time the area north of the Ohio River and west of the Allegheny Mountains was part of British North America, not the American colonies, and with Butler's Rangers, Pawpine fought the Americans by waging a fierce and cruel guerrilla-style campaign from the Hudson to the Kentucky Rivers to interrupt the supply routes of the Continental army.

In July 1784, a year after the war ended, he left the army, a seasoned veteran of forty-six, and disappeared from the pages of history again for four years. He probably stayed in the area working as a laborer or farmhand, because in 1788 he was granted, as a veteran, a two-hundred-acre parcel of land on Twelve-Mile Creek, near present-day St. Catharines, Ontario. He worked for three years to clear the land and build a dwelling—required as a condition of the grant—and in January 1791, Lots 13 and 14, Concession 6, became his property. He later sold them. Why? Turning forest into a farm was dangerous, painstaking, backbreaking work. Why go to all that trouble, then sell off the farm?

The Niagara Frontier was populated by Iroquois, Dutch, Jews, Scots, Germans and many expatriate Americans loyal to Britain, but few Africans. The government was lily-white and undemocratic, and so was high society. Pawpine, a veteran and a landowner, was still an outsider. He felt that he didn't belong, that he was unwelcome.

Ms. Song, right now you're asking, how does Zack know that? My answer is that in 1794 Pawpine and a number of other free Africans petitioned Governor John G. Simcoe. Who were they? Veterans of the "late War and others who were born free with a few who have come into Canada since the peace." What did they request? They were "desirous of settling adjacent to each other in order that they may be able to give assistance in work to those amongst them who may most want it." They asked the governor "to allow them a Tract of County to settle on, separate from the white settlers." Why would they make a request like that if they had been a part of things?

The governor said no.

To make matters worse the next governor, Peter Hunter, removed Pawpine's name from the list of United Empire Loyalists. After 1806, Pawpine, who had fought the Americans for the king, was no longer considered a "loyalist." Why? I think it was because he was African.

Six years passed, and there is no record of him. In 1812 the Americans got mad at the British again and invaded Canada, trying to grab more land, as if half a continent wasn't enough. And guess who turned up to enlist?

No longer a landowner in Grantham Township, he wasn't some young guy looking for adventure or itching to get off the farm and carry a gun. He was sixty-eight years old. He wrote to the authorities offering to "raise a Corps of Men of Colour on the Niagara Frontier." "No, thanks," the British said. But when a British captain named Runchey agreed to lead the thirty or so Africans, assent was given. We'll let you fight, the British said to Pawpine, but you can't lead.

It might have been one of the stupidest wars ever fought, so full of blunders and gaffes it would have been comical if so many hadn't been killed. Pawpine was in the thick of it—the siege of Fort George, the battles of Lundy's Lane and of Queenston Heights. Henry Clay had told the American Congress in February 1810 that "the militia of Kentucky alone" could take Montreal and Upper Canada both. He must have been embarrassed when he learned that part of Washington was burned down and that the Redcoats invaded as far as New Orleans. The Americans won the last battle in 1815—two weeks after the peace terms had been negotiated and the war ended. Most of the war had been fought on Canadian soil. Not a single acre of land changed hands.

Pawpine's name is on the papers that officially disbanded Runchey's "Coloured Corps" in 1815. He went back to scratching a living as a laborer and slipped out of sight for another six years.

When he was seventy-seven years old, Pawpine was living in Niagara-on-the-Lake, a lonely old man with no family and few friends. Vouched for by the adjutant general of militia, who praised the service in two wars of "a faithful and deserving old Negro," he petitioned Lieutenant Governor Maitland on July 21, 1821: "Old and without property," he found it "extremely hard to obtain a livelihood by my labour."

What did he ask for? Land? Money? A job? No.

"Desirous above all things to return to my native country," he requested a ticket home to Africa.

Pawpine got a ticket, all right—a "location ticket" for a parcel of unbroken wilderness land a hundred miles as the crow flies from Niagara-on-the-Lake, with the usual conditions—clear the land, build a house.

It took four years, but he did it. His cabin was built on the bank of the Grand River. If it was still there it would be standing in my yard, right behind my house. I live on his farm.

As he sat in his cabin door gazing over the gray frozen river at fields of snow, how could he not dream of the hot steamy Gambia, of his village and family and friends? I wonder if he recalled stories and songs, if he even remembered his language. He came to North America alone, and he died alone eleven years after he cleared his land. He was more than ninety years old.

Some time before he died he took his leather-covered document box and inside it he placed his old Butler's Ranger shoulder straps. He must have been proud to be a ranger. He wrapped his slave's collar in greased leather and put it into the box too. Why had he kept the collar? Because it was a link to his boyhood? He then added his bit of gold and buried the box where my mother's lilac bushes now grow.

Ms. Song, whenever we finish a unit, you always give us a test. You want to know what we learned.

Although he spent his life in a strange land, I'm certain that in his own mind Pawpine was always an African. He never gave up, never bowed his head to anyone, and never, never forgot who he was or where he came from.

I wasn't born in Africa, but my mother's

ancestors were. They were taken from their homes, they survived the middle passage, they lived and died, had families, worked hard.

I know it sounds crazy, Ms. Song, but I feel linked to Pawpine, as if he was part of my family. He gave me something I never thought I had. And his bit of gold is like a gift that was waiting all those years for me to find it.

I have a plan that I haven't told anyone about yet, and the gold will help me carry it out. I think he would have been pleased.

THE END

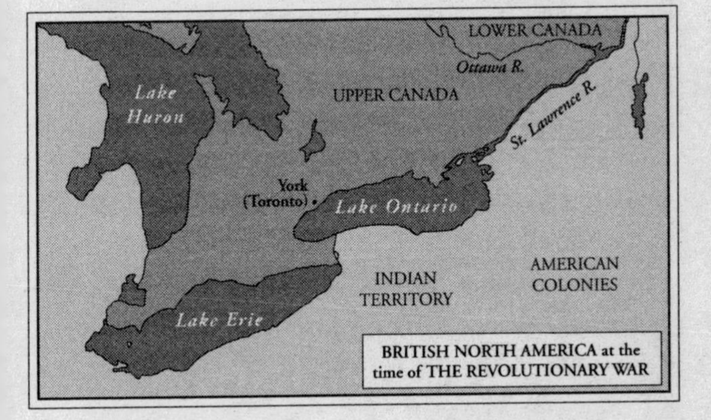

BRITISH NORTH AMERICA at the time of THE REVOLUTIONARY WAR

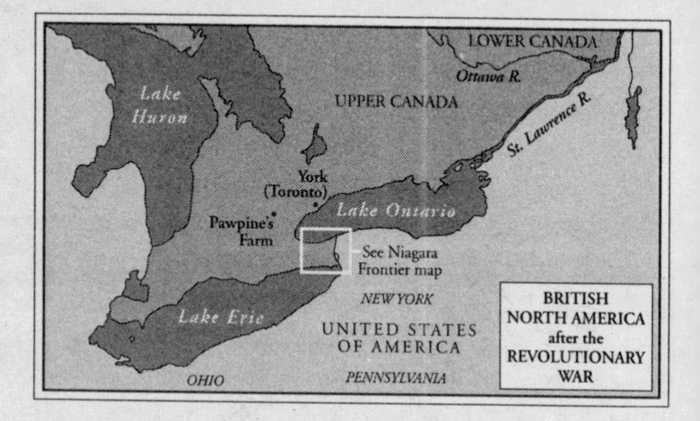
LOWER CANADA
Ottawa R.
Lake Huron
UPPER CANADA
St. Lawrence R.
York (Toronto)
Lake Ontario
Pawpine's Farm
See Niagara Frontier map
NEW YORK
Lake Erie
UNITED STATES OF AMERICA
OHIO
PENNSYLVANIA
BRITISH NORTH AMERICA after the REVOLUTIONARY WAR

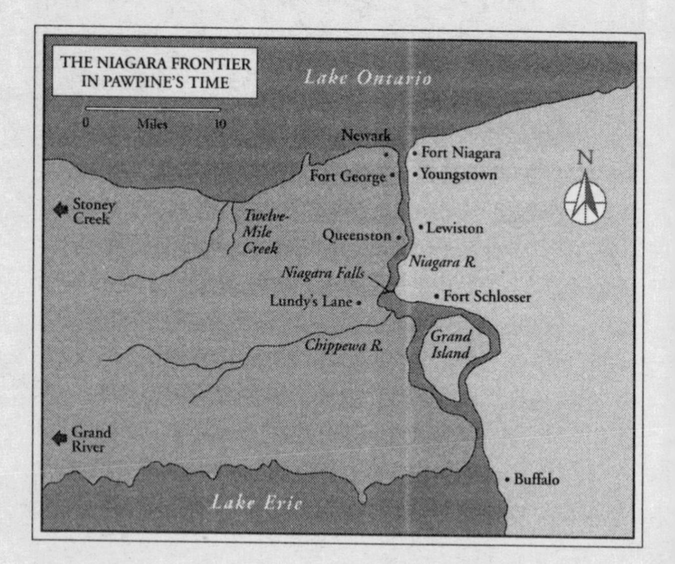
THE NIAGARA FRONTIER IN PAWPINE'S TIME
Lake Ontario
0 Miles 10
Newark
Fort Niagara
Fort George
Youngstown
N
Stoney Creek
Twelve-Mile Creek
Queenston
Lewiston
Niagara R.
Niagara Falls
Lundy's Lane
Fort Schlosser
Grand Island
Chippewa R.
Grand River
Buffalo
Lake Erie

PART THREE

I did have a plan. But I also had a few problems. The scheme came to mind after Mom told me that she had a ten-day gig in Montreal at the Maple Leaf Blues Festival, and that Dad was going too. He hated it when she was away for more than a couple of days. When Mom asked if I'd like to go along, it hit me: While they were gone I could take a trip of my own. So I told her no thanks.

Since my visit to the Wellington County Museum, I had done a lot of heavy thinking. Probably nothing looked different on the outside, but inside I felt myself changing. It sounds strange, but when Knox gave me the news about the half rings I felt ashamed and humiliated, as if I had been diminished somehow. I had never given much thought to the fact that my ancestors on Mom's side had been slaves not many generations ago.

For the next few days I had been pretty confused. I'd feel low, then get mad at myself—why should I feel bad? I'd ask—then get angry at everyone. Dad thought I was worried about school. Mom raised her eyebrows at me when I grouched at her and gave me one of her patented understanding looks that drove me nuts. Jen told me more than once that she was the only female in the county that would put up with me.

But by the time I had finished my research on Pawpine I was proud of my African forebears. Maybe they didn't have a coat of arms, maybe there were no towns named after them, but, like Grandpa had said about the Lazarovitches, they had made a place to stand on.

I wanted to get to know my maternal grandfather and meet my American relatives, and the only way I could hook up with them was to go to Natchez, Mississippi.

But I couldn't tell my parents. Any hint to Mom that I wanted to contact my grandfather would be like throwing a bucket of water on a gasoline fire. Not to mention the fact that my parents would never agree to let me take a trip alone in the family pickup truck.

It took a lot of persuasion, with many reminders that I wasn't a kindergarten kid incapable of taking care of myself for a week or so, before Mom and Dad agreed that it wasn't necessary to send me to live with my grandparents during their absence. I pretended that I didn't want to be away from Jen—which was true, except I didn't tell them that Jen was flying with her parents to Calgary for two weeks.

My last problem was a biggie—money. I had maybe sixty or seventy bucks in a bank account saved from cash birthday gifts and odd jobs, but I would need a lot more than that for gas and food and stuff. I didn't have to think very hard before I came up with the solution.

When I entered the jewelry store Mr. Piffard was in his chair behind the counter reading a newspaper, glasses perched on the end of his prominent nose. A cup with a tea-bag string hanging out of it sat on the glass beside the oblong of red velvet.

He looked up when the bell tinkled and his cigar migrated in jumps from one corner of his mouth to the other.

"Afternoon," he said.

"Hi, Mr. Piffard."

"Nice day."

"Er, yeah," I agreed, fingering the gold nugget in my pocket. "Really nice. Sunny. Nice and sunny."

I would have gone on with more of the same babble and made a bigger fool of myself but he interrupted.

"What can I do for you?"

I placed the gold on the velvet. "I came to take you up on your offer to buy this from me."

Beside it I laid a forged letter. Jen had written the note giving me permission to sell Pawpine's gold and signed it with my father's name.

"It's too neat," I had told her when she had presented me with the first version. "Dad's a university prof. You can hardly read his writing."

Jen had tossed her hair in agitation. "Then why not do it on the word processor and I'll just sign his name?"

"Because it has to look as if he jotted it down quickly, like it's not that big a deal."

"Then why don't *you* write it?"

"What, and do something dishonest?"

Jen had balled up the letter and bounced it off my nose. It had taken two more drafts to get it right.

Mr. Piffard scanned the paper. "This is your father's phone number?"

"He can be reached there during office hours."

That was only half a lie. It was the modem number, in use most of the day. If the jeweler called he'd get a busy signal—that was what I was counting on.

"You're sure you want to sell this thing?"

"Well, er, pretty sure. No, yes I do."

"All right, then."

I left the shop with almost four hundred dollars in my pocket. As soon as the door clicked shut behind me I knew I'd made a colossal mistake. I had sold off a precious piece of history, a link with the man I had come to admire so much I felt that I knew him. The gold would be melted and made into a trinket, forever lost.

I turned back, put my hand on the door handle. The bell sounded once more. Mr. Piffard was not in the shop. Thoughts flashed in my mind. Get the nugget back, now! No, keep the money. The nugget is priceless. But I needed the cash. The gold was a gift so I could do what I had to do.

The curtain at the back moved. A hand appeared, pushing it aside. I turned and ran from the shop.

On the last Friday of June, I hoped my eagerness to get Mom and Dad out of my hair didn't show. Although their plane didn't leave until eleven o'clock, Dad was up at six, clanging and banging around, overorganizing things and tripping over his own feet.

The night before, Mom had packed three guitars into their hard cases—the electric, her favorite six-string, and, "in case some old-timers want to jam folksy," her twelve-string—and one suitcase for clothes. Her toiletries she stuffed into a backpack at the last minute, along with a few novels and her sunglasses. She was a veteran traveler.

You'd never have known it by Dad's peppering her with questions. Should we bring this? Did you pack that? He had two suitcases containing everything from his laptop to exams to mark to journals he wanted to catch up on, along with enough clothes to outfit a platoon for a month.

The last thing he did really burned me. Without even making a secret of it, he copied down the odometer reading from the pickup. He wanted me to know I wasn't to use the truck too much. Get ready for a big surprise when you come home, Dad, I thought.

We loaded the whole catastrophe into the back of the truck and headed for the airport. An hour and a half later Dad pulled up to the curb on the departure deck under the watchful eye of a Mountie who looked at us as if we were shipping bags of cocaine back to Colombia for a refund.

"Be careful," was all Dad said as he loaded the gear onto a cart.

"Now, we're trusting you to act sensibly while we're gone, Zack," Mom told me for the tenth time. "Don't let us down."

"Yes, Mom."

"Remember to turn out all the lights and lock the doors when you leave the house. And don't leave dirty dishes around."

"Yes, Mom."

"And water the plants. Give the lilacs and the flowers in the yard a good soaking."

"Yes, Mom."

She kissed me and laughed. "I'll bet you wish I'd shut up and get on the plane."

"Yes, Mom."

"All right. We're leaving. Bye, dear."

"Bye, Mom. Bye, Dad."

I watched them push the cart through the automatic doors and heaved a sigh of relief. As I drove off I even waved to the Mountie.

The first thing I did when I got back to town was hit the supermarket, where I bought two cases of apple juice in small bottles and a case of tonic water—sue me, I don't like cola—three boxes of soda crackers, a big jar of crunchy peanut butter, three blocks of cheddar cheese, half a dozen packs of sliced meat and two bags of ice cubes for the cooler. At the Canadian Tire store I picked up a Canada/U.S. road atlas, a plastic rain poncho, some bug lotion, and sunblock. Next stop, the bank, to buy American dollars.

Back home, I packed the food into the fridge and tossed the cubes into the freezer chest. In a trunk in the cellar I located Dad's old sleeping bag and took it out into the yard to air out in the sun. I removed the thick foam mattress from one of the chaise longues on the patio and retrieved a pillow from my room. Sleeping accommodations done.

I stuffed enough clothes for a week into a flight bag Mom never used, threw in a couple of detective novels from the bookshelves in the living room, added my portable CD player and some discs, and headed for the garage.

Suspended from the rafters by a series of pulleys and ropes that only my father could have devised was a truck cap he had bought at a garage sale and used once—on the way home from the garage sale. It took half an hour and a lot of cursing and knuckle skinning to get the cap onto the Toyota and locked in place. The truck's box was now a weatherproof compartment accessed by a tiny door at the back.

I realized afterward that it would have been a good idea to pack my gear into the Toyota before I installed the cap. Grumbling to myself about my own stupidity,

I swept out the compartment and put in the mattress and bedding. The rest of the stuff could wait until morning.

In the kitchen I put the kettle on while I made a list, then assembled more stuff—the cooler, a flashlight, Mom's extra long-distance calling card (she kept it in a kitchen drawer)—and last but most important, I rummaged through my desk for a Christmas card sent to us years before. I had retrieved it from the garbage when Mom wasn't looking. My uncle had written my grandfather's address inside it, hoping, I guess, that Mom would relent and write to him. Fat chance.

I fired up Dad's computer and ran off a copy of my Pawpine research paper, which I added to the pile of stuff on the kitchen table. While I sipped my tea, I consulted the road atlas and planned my route. Then I began to water Mom's ten thousand houseplants before I turned the garden hose on the lilacs and her little flower farm in the yard.

"So, are you going to miss me?" I asked.

"Don't talk with your mouth full," Jen said. "And, no, I won't miss you. Soon as I get to Calgary I'll go to a bar and find a guy with a cowboy hat, tight jeans, and a nice butt." She wiped ketchup from the corner of her lips and added, "Are you going to miss me? Or is the excitement of this illegal and crazy trip of yours too much?"

"I wish you could come with me."

"So do I, Zack. But I'd just get in your way."

"Yeah, sure."

"Did anyone ever tell you that you look sexy with pizza sauce on your chin?"

"I've been waiting for you to notice."

"Come here," she said.

I have never been a morning person. Although I had set the alarm for six-thirty it was nine before I hauled myself out of bed, rubbed the sleep from my eyes, showered, and dressed. After Jen had left the night before, I had lain awake listening to the breeze outside my open window and the Grand River flowing along, wondering if the whole idea of the trip was a mistake. It was late before I fell asleep.

After a breakfast of toast and coffee I packed up all the gear and stowed it in the truck, then I did a tour of the house, checking to make sure all the windows and doors were locked, the timers set on the upstairs and downstairs lights, and the water main in the basement was shut off. It was ten o'clock when I pulled out of Fergus and headed south on Highway 6, my atlas open beside me on the seat.

I followed 6 into Hamilton, stopped at a doughnut shop to use the bathroom and pick up a coffee, and lost half an hour tearing up and down one-way streets, cursing and trying to find the Queen Elizabeth Way. The highway was thick with cars whose drivers seemed bent on killing themselves and each other, along with hundreds of huge transport trucks that looked eager to help. Unused to driving on big roads, I gripped the steering wheel and kept the Toyota in the right lane, buffeted by powerful draughts from the passing trucks. At St. Catharines I kept my eye open and when I saw the sign for Twelve-Mile Creek I pulled over onto the shoulder.

I hadn't known what to expect. What greeted me was pretty unexciting—a sluggish stream winding through a flat, unremarkable landscape before it slipped under the ugly concrete tangle of the highway, which howled with traffic. I tried, without success, to imagine what the creek looked like a century and a half before, when Pawpine pioneered his homestead there.

Instead of crossing at Niagara Falls I followed the signs for Queenston and drove past the statue of General Brock, big hero of the Battle of Queenston Heights who was killed fending off the American invasion in 1812. Pawpine may have fought there too. No statue for him, though.

I paid the toll and drove over the bridge that spanned the Niagara River, thundering and boiling on its way north to Lake Ontario. Behind a huge motor home from Texas I came to a stop at the row of customs booths. When the motor home moved off I drove up to the booth and rolled down my window. The agent studied me behind mirror aviator sunglasses and spoke in a bored monotone.

"Citizenship?"

"Canadian."

"How long do you plan to stay in the United States?"

"A week or so."

I wondered why he needed sunglasses sitting in a dimly lit enclosure under a shaded roof. His next question threw me.

"What's your destination?"

"Er, Natchez."

"Where's that?"

Was this a test? I wondered. Or was this guy's knowledge of geography as dim as his eyesight?

"In Mississippi," I said.

So far, I had felt like I was under arrest as each question came harsher than the last.

"What's the purpose of your visit?"

To pick up a ton of heroin and a nuclear warhead, I felt like saying, but something told me that he had a severe irony deficiency.

"I'm going to visit my grandfather."

The agent adjusted his sunglasses. "You got proof of ownership for that truck?" he asked.

I stretched across the seat and rummaged around in the glove compartment amid road maps and used-up ballpoint pens until I found the small blue plastic folder Dad used to keep the ownership and insurance slip. I handed it over. The agent examined the papers carefully before handing back the folder. But he wasn't done with me.

"What's your grandfather's address?"

I passed across my uncle's Christmas card. The agent turned it over, read the inside, then peered at the stamp on the envelope as if he suspected it was counterfeit. He gave it back.

With the warmth of an iguana he said, "Enjoy your stay."

I threw the truck into gear and pulled away, turning onto Highway 190. The city of Buffalo seemed to be having a pothole competition with someplace. I got to the New York State Thruway and turned west, stopping for gas at the first station. The highway was straight, flat, and boring. At Erie I took Interstate 79 South toward Pittsburgh.

By then it was late afternoon. If the road west was dull, this one was worse, pushing through flat, featureless farmland. I was learning that what the interstates offered in convenience and travel time they balanced with boredom. Driving along, I seemed to be sitting stationary on a conveyor belt, other cars and trucks scattered around me, pulled through the countryside at a steady numbing pace.

Near Pittsburgh the terrain became hilly. I bypassed the city and turned west again on I-70. At the Ohio border I stopped at a "welcome station," which introduced me to the state with washrooms, vending machines, and racks of pamphlets advertising motels, tourist attractions, stores, and other hot spots.

I pulled up in the nearly empty parking area and shut off the truck. After I stretched my legs and twisted the kinks out of my spine, I fished my long-distance calling card out of my wallet and walked to the bank of pay phones. It was time to set Operation Deception in motion.

I placed a call to my house. The phone rang only twice before the answering machine picked up, indicating that a message had been left. It was Dad, telling me their hotel's phone number and room number. I jotted down the information on the corner of a page I tore out of the phone book.

Our answering machine could be programmed from a phone. When it was clear Dad's was the only message, I used the telephone keypad to erase his message. Then I erased the outgoing message, punched in another code number, and held my fingers over the receiver.

Pitching my voice as high as I could, I said in a nasal monotone, "I'm sorry. This number is not in service."

Pleased with the detective-novel ruse, I hung up and redialed, using the calling card again. Sure enough, the phone rang four times, the machine picked up, and I heard myself tell me that our phone didn't work. So far, so good. Squinting at my scribbled note, I called my parents' hotel in Montreal and asked to leave a message for Mr. and Mrs. Lane.

"Shall I connect you to their room?" the receptionist asked.

"No, just take the message, please."

"Very well. You may record your message when you hear the beep."

I reported that our phone was acting up. I said Grandpa had tried to call a few times and got a "not in service" message. "So I'll call you every couple of days, Mom. Don't worry, everything's fine. Bye," I ended cheerily.

One more call to make.

"Hello."

"Hi, Grandma. It's Zack."

"Hello, dear. How are you?"

"Oh, fine. Just watching the tube, you know. Um, I called to tell you and Grandpa that there's something wrong with our phone. I can call out but people can't call in."

"That's strange."

"Yeah, isn't it, though? Anyway, I'll be in touch with you every couple of days, okay?"

"Yes, dear, but—"

"Oh, jeez, the kettle's boiling. Gotta run, Grandma. Talk to you later, bye!"

I hung up quickly, no longer puffed up with my trickery. Fibbing to a machine was one thing. Tricking my grandma was something else.

I climbed into the back of the truck, opened the cooler, made myself a sandwich of ham, cheese, and peanut butter, and took it to a picnic table under the trees beside the building. Long shadows striped the parking area and the air was cooling down. As I ate, cars pulled up, travelers walked to and from the comfort station, sat in their cars consulting maps, drove off again. It was a lonely place. Nobody knew anybody else—didn't want to know. They left the familiar interior of their vehicles for a short excursion and returned as quickly as possible, closing and locking the doors, safe again.

The food made me drowsy and I felt my eyelids droop as I sat on the hard seat thinking those profound thoughts. I climbed into the cab of the Toyota and curled up in the front seat. Just a short nap, I told myself, then I'll get going.

When I woke up, cramped and a little chilly, it was dark out and the condensation on the windshield blurred the light coming from the building, giving me the sense that I was under amber-colored water. A slight headache throbbed behind my ears and my mouth was sticky. In the rearview mirror I saw the yellow dots of light along the top of a transport truck. There seemed to be no one else around.

The clock on the dashboard read 12:42. I pulled the keys from the ignition, locked the cab, and crawled into the back. Carelessly I kicked off my shoes. I crawled into the sleeping bag, burrowed deep, and went back to sleep.

I dreamed I was trapped in an underwater cave, drowning in white light that burned through my eyelids. I thrashed in panic, desperate to escape. Groaning with fear, I rolled onto my stomach and pulled the sleeping bag over my head. Darkness fell and I could breathe again. Then came deep hollow voices, the scrape of leather boots on concrete.

" . . . in here," a voice said—male, straining with tension.

A fist pounded on a door. It was my door. It was the door of the truck cap.

I snatched the covers from my face and bolted to my knees. The rear window of the truck was an explosion of piercing white light. Blinded, I shielded my eyes with my arm.

A second voice, muffled, deeper than the first. "I see him!"

The door thumped and rattled as the fist struck it again. My heartbeats throbbed in my head as I scrambled for my clothes, as if pulling on my jeans would stop the terror that dried my mouth. I remembered news reports from last winter, stories of tourists in Florida murdered for their cash on the edge of the Interstates. Frantically I groped around for something I could use as a weapon, knowing I was trapped. My fingers closed on the handle of the knife I had used to make my sandwich.

Behind the glare of light a voice boomed. "You in there! Come out now!"

The door handle rattled. I had locked it when I had climbed in. I turned away from the blazing window and looked through the cab out the front of the truck to see a looming shape, a moving light. Behind me, the door thundered.

"This is the Highway Patrol. Put down your weapon! Come out of the truck with your hands on your head. Now!"

At first I felt a wave of relief. Cops. I was safe. Then, fear again. What if they weren't cops at all? I couldn't see them. Momentarily I considered waiting them out. I was trapped, yes, but they couldn't get in.

"How do I know you're police?" I yelled.

For an instant the light disappeared from the window and shone on a human shape. A badge gleamed, then the light returned, full into my face.

"Come out!" the voice boomed. "Keep your hands in sight."

I dropped the knife and shuffled on my knees, hands held out before me like a beggar. I reached to slide back the bolt on the door.

"I said keep your hands in sight!"

"It's locked," I said, surprised at the firmness of my voice.

"Put your right hand on your head. Unlock with your left."

I did as he told me. My fear had lessened, but not by much. The door flew open and a hand the size of a catcher's mitt closed on my shoulder, bunching my T-shirt. Fingers dug painfully. I was dragged out the door so violently that I couldn't get my feet under me. I fell headlong to the pavement, striking my head, and a new burst of light blazed behind my eyes. The air exploded from my lungs when my chest hit the ground. Dazed, I felt my arms pulled behind me. A knee ground into my back, the skin on my wrists pinched and I heard two loud clicks.

The cops lifted me to my feet and slammed me against the side of the truck. A light was trained on my eyes.

"Where are the keys?"

"In my back pocket," I gasped. I could hardly breathe.

A hand was thrust into my pocket. My keys jingled. The truck door was opened and noises told me the second cop was searching the cab.

"Could you put that light down, please?" I said. "You're hurting my eyes."

The glare dropped away and I blinked the sparkles away from my eyeballs. When my vision returned I found myself facing a very large man wearing a Smokey the Bear hat, unzipped windbreaker, leather belt with gun in holster and nightstick dangling. His face was round and fleshy and his breath stank of cigarettes.

"Where's your ID?" he said.

"My wallet's in my back pocket."

"Turn around."

The cop jerked my wallet from my jeans and ordered me to face front. He checked my driver's license and student card.

"Nothing here, Duane," the second cop called from the cab.

"Look in the back."

My wallet was stuffed back into my pocket. The big cop grabbed me under the arm, lifting me enough to keep me off balance, and hauled me to the cruiser. Its engine was running but the lights were off. The rear door squeaked as the cop pulled it open and shoved me head first into the car, so hard I sprawled across the edge of the seat then fell onto the floor, my face burning when it rubbed against the carpeting, my shoulders pinched back as I was squeezed into the narrow space between the front and back seats. The door struck my feet when he closed it. A front door opened and the car sagged when the cop got in.

A nauseating stench of puke, sweat, and old shoes

filled my nostrils. I breathed through my mouth, fighting down the heaves. A ball of fiery pain burned between my shoulders and I strove to hold off claustrophobic panic as I lay face down, wrists manacled behind me.

The cop was talking into the radio mike. Computer keys clicked. A few moments later he got out, opened the back door, and helped me out of the car.

"Didn't you see the sign?" he asked, the tough edge gone from his voice. "It's illegal to camp here."

"Yeah, but I didn't mean to sleep so long."

I was tempted to point out that the truck down the parking lot had been there longer than I had, but I kept my mouth shut.

"Nothing in his truck, Duane," the second cop said. He was a clone of the first cop, except his jacket was zipped up and he had a pencil mustache.

"Listen, fella," Duane said. "Aside from the bylaw, it's not a good idea to camp out in a place like this. There's a lotta mean types riding the Interstate. You wanna catch some sleep, go to a campground."

"We gonna write him up?" Mustache said, turning off his flashlight.

"Where you headed?" Duane asked me.

"Mississippi. I'm going to visit my grandfather."

"Turn around."

With a jingle the cuffs fell away.

"We're gonna let you go with a warning. But watch yourself. Don't do anything foolish like this again."

"Yessir," I said.

The two cops walked slowly to the cruiser and got

in. Duane spoke into his mike as Moustache drove away.

I got into the Toyota and pushed the key into the ignition. The contents of the glove compartment were strewn across the seat and littered the floor. I felt liquid trickle down one side of my nose and into my mouth. I tasted blood. When I reached to the floor for the box of tissues I noticed the scrapes on my wrists where the manacles had dug in.

I started the truck and steered onto the Interstate, a pain stabbing my shoulders each time I changed gears. As I drove I dabbed the cut on my aching head with the bloody tissue.

By dawn, Columbus was behind me and I was headed toward Cincinnati on I-71. My hands still shook if I took them off the wheel.

A little while after I crossed the Kentucky border I saw a familiar name: General Butler State Park. He couldn't have been the Butler from Pawpine's days in the Revolutionary War, but I took the off ramp anyway and followed the two-lane black-top through the hills. I figured I'd find a campsite, put the truck back in order—the cop who searched it had low respect for other people's property—and take it easy for the rest of the day. Getting handcuffed and thrown around and generally treated like a crook had tired me out.

The sun was high in the sky when I located the campsite assigned to me by the ranger. It was in a row of sites along a creek that, according to my map, trickled through the hardwoods into the Kentucky River. The campground wasn't full—the sites on both sides of me were unoccupied—but it wasn't like being out in the wilderness either. Dogs barked, kids flashed past on mountain bikes, car engines growled to life, savory blue smoke from barbecues drifted on the hot air.

I sat on the picnic table munching a three-decker sandwich and sipping tonic water from the can, watching a pair of ducks tip their tail feathers toward the clear blue sky as they fed and chuckled in the shallows. A light breeze murmured in the evergreens that flanked my campsite. But I couldn't relax.

I didn't really feel like reliving the experience at the welcome station but I knew I had to. Mom had always told me never to hold down feelings or pretend they weren't there. "If you do," she'd say, "those emotions will stew and bubble like a volcano and sooner or later they'll erupt, usually when you don't expect it. Yeah," she added, mixing her metaphor, "like thugs crashing a party."

Well, a thug was what I felt like. What had that whole SWAT team episode been all about, anyway? A kid trapped in the back of a pickup truck wasn't exactly a terrorist threat. The cop who had cuffed me and thrown me into the cruiser had either taken too many steroids or watched too much TV. And his partner. Thrashing around in my truck, pulling my belongings apart, poring over everything I owned, leaving a chaotic mess behind him.

I fingered the wound on my forehead; it was still sticky and it stung when I touched it. I drank down the last of my tonic water and flung the can at the garbage drum chained to a hardwood tree, then pounded the top of the picnic table, seething in frustration. Manacled and disoriented, I had felt completely helpless against the authority and menace of the two cops. It was hard to explain: They had treated me like scum, and for that reason I felt worthless, a nothing, and when the cop had hauled me out of the cruiser and unlocked the cuffs I had felt *grateful.* Now I was disgusted with myself for letting them get to me that way.

I hopped off the table, picked up the can, and dropped it into the drum. I climbed into the truck and changed into my running gear. After I locked up, I loped off down the gravel road and jogged around the park to warm up before I came to the hill by the main gate. Leaning into the ascent, I sprinted to the crest, turned and jogged back down, dashed to the top again, repeated the cycle endlessly, grinding up the steep grade again and again until sweat streamed from every pore, my chest rose and collapsed like a bellows, my pulse hammered in my ears, my thigh muscles burned and quivered. I pounded up that hill until I crumpled exhausted to the grass by the side of the road.

The hangover from my running fell on me like a bag of sand, sending me into a dreamless sleep. I woke slapping mosquitoes and perspiring: The inside of the truck was like a stove. I crawled out into the morning swelter, grabbed my gear and headed along the road to the showers. I might as well have saved my energy. By the time I got back to the campsite every inch of my frame was bathed in sweat.

After a gourmet breakfast of peanut butter and crackers washed down with warm apple juice, I decamped. Above me a gray slab of sky threatened rain. I hit Louisville just in time to get snarled in rush-hour traffic on the bypass that looped around the city to connect with I-65. Blasted by humid air rushing in the windows, I drove south, set my watch back an hour at Upton. The highway seemed to sway between the hills like a pendulum. Kentucky blended into Tennessee, and not long after, I made Nashville. No fan of country music and its variations, I kept the radio silent, and as if in revenge the tangle of intersecting highways and bypasses around the city led me the wrong way. Instead of slipping past the music capital I found myself in it, and then the rain began.

Exasperated and short-tempered, I pulled into a mini-mall, bought a vacuum flask, and got it filled with coffee at a take-out chicken joint. In an accent as thick as molasses the waiter gave me directions, drawing a crude map on a napkin while he drawled away, his Adam's apple bobbing. Talking to him, I knew I was finally in the South, and my trip to see my grandfather, for so long an abstract plan, began to feel real.

Fifteen minutes later I was speeding south on Highway 100, looking for a place called Pasquo. By the time I found the little town the rain was heavy and thick and I almost missed the sign indicating the northern terminus of the Natchez Trace Parkway. I parked in the lot, went inside the welcome center and left a few moments later with a collection of booklets and a map, which I looked over in the truck, sipping hot strong coffee.

"You're goin' to Natchez, you oughta take the Trace," the waiter had suggested, completely confusing me until he explained that the Trace was a five-hundred-mile-long two-lane road. Looking at the map, I could see his advice was good. I was sick to death of the homogenized boredom of the interstates.

The Parkway began just outside Nashville and twisted and bent its way south through Tennessee, taking a twenty-five-mile bite out of Alabama before crossing into Mississippi.

Reading the pamphlets while the rain drummed on the roof and coursed down the fogged windshield, I felt like a time traveler. For centuries before Columbus landed in the so-called New World (to the millions of people already living here it was the same old place), the Trace had been a major trail used by Choctaw and Chickasaw Indians. Later, Hernando de Soto—whoever he was, I thought, imagining a frown of displeasure on The Book's chubby face—had followed it. So had the explorer Meriwether Lewis and the Indian killer and someday president Andrew Jackson. The Trace became a post road after 1800. Most of the travelers, settlers, and merchants who floated their wares on timber barges down the Mississippi River to Natchez, sold the boats because they couldn't be poled back upriver against the current, and then hiked back north on the Trace.

In a strange sort of way I thought the ancient trail was part of my history too. "None of you came from nowhere," The Book had told us in our first class the previous February, smiling at our confusion. "That's a *correct* use of a double negative. All of you came from somewhere. You have a history. This subject isn't an abstract list of dates and wars and constitutions. It's real. As real as you are."

I read that the Trace would take me past farms and fields where slaves had bent sweating over rows of vegetables and cotton with crude hoes in their callused hands. Yeah, I thought, men and women like Pawpine whose parents and grandparents had been torn from their lives and homes in Africa, shipped across the sea, given strange names, and put to work building a country they weren't allowed to share in.

I turned the window defroster on high, spread the map open beside me on the seat and started the truck. When the windshield cleared I turned south again.

I didn't get far. The road, a well-maintained two-lane with wide grassy shoulders, wove its way through gently rolling woods that opened up occasionally into farmland. The rain beat down with a vengeance and thunder growled in the distance. I passed Garrison Creek, pushed on until I got to a picnic area with a sign that said "Old Trace," and finally gave in, pulling off the road. The windshield wipers flapped in vain against the sheets of water pouring down. At the far edge of the little parking lot a bush road led to a hiking trail. Remembering the cops in Ohio, I steered the truck into the bush until it was out of sight.

The few steps from the cab to the back door were enough for the roaring rain to drench me to the skin. Inside, I pulled off my wet clothes and tossed them into a corner. I clicked on my flashlight and lay down on the sleeping bag, head propped up on my clothes pack, and read a mystery novel, slapping mosquitoes that hummed in the humid air before taking turns at the feast.

Some time during the night I woke to the roar of

wind, the drumming of rain, and the hollow slamming of branches striking the top and sides of the truck. With the violence of a ship striking a reef, a thunderclap burst overhead. I sat up quickly, banging my head on the rear wall of the cab as I scrambled to my knees. I peered out the back window just as a flash of lightning crackled for at least two seconds, illuminating the parking lot and the meadow with a ghostly blue light. A deafening crack of thunder followed immediately. The storm was right above me, flinging sheets of rain against the truck. The wind came in furious waves. Another blinding bolt of lightning leaped from the dark sea of sky, driving me from the window just as thunder slammed the air and the floor shuddered under me. A second later, something exploded behind me and crashed down, rocking the truck on its springs like a toy boat.

I dove under my sleeping bag and rolled into a ball, wishing the storm would go away. Two more flashes lit up the sky, so bright the light pierced my bedding; two more eruptions of sound pounded above me before I realized the tumult was receding. As slow as a tide, the wind lessened in power and the deluge became rain again.

I'd like to say that I jumped out of the truck eager to do battle with the forces of nature and anxious to survey the damage, but I stayed inside, shaking and wide-eyed until dawn. I dressed in shorts and a T-shirt and climbed out of the truck onto the spongy leaf-covered track. Gray light and birdsong filled the bush around me and gold sunlight tinged the treetops along the edge of the meadow. It was already hot, the air sodden with moisture.

Pushing fallen branches aside, I made my way to the front of the truck. A monstrous dead oak had crashed down in the storm, crushing dozens of smaller trees as it fell, and its topmost branches had grazed the Toyota's hood and fender. The hood was creased across the middle, the fender was crumpled and one headlight smashed.

"Man-oh-man," I muttered. The massive trunk of the oak, almost two feet in diameter, had broken off about six feet above the ground. Had I parked a few yards farther into the bush the tree would have struck the truck's cap, crushing both it and me into the muddy ground.

"Welcome to Mississippi, Zack," I said out loud.

I wished I could have lit a bonfire to cheer myself up, but even an experienced woodsman would have been challenged to coax a flame from the drenched wood scattered around me. I sat down on the rear bumper of the truck. There had been times in my life—like the time I had given in to the nagging of a girl I had been going out with in ninth grade and tried marijuana—when I had shaken my head in disgust and asked myself, Zack, what the hell are you doing? This was one of those times.

I had lied to my parents and grandparents, taken the family wheels without permission, almost gotten myself arrested and my head broken, smashed up the truck—and for what? To find a grandfather my mother wouldn't talk to for reasons I didn't know. It began to look like living in Fergus had ruined my brain after all.

I sipped some lukewarm coffee left over from the day before and dabbed the cut in my forehead—it had begun to bleed again when I cracked it against the truck wall during the storm—while I thought about my options. It didn't take long. I had only two choices. I could continue my goofy quest or I could point the truck north and go home. Maybe, I thought, I could get back in time to get the truck repaired before my parents returned and pretend nothing had happened. That idea died with the first mosquito of the morning as it tried to bore a hole in my forearm. I hadn't really thought about the net result of leaving home, but I had known I'd really be in for it, regardless of the condition of the truck. They would find out. That was clear.

And besides, if I slunk back to Fergus I would have nothing to justify my lies and mistakes. My only hope was the remote possibility that no matter what punishment was eventually laid on me I could tell myself it was worth it because I had met my grandfather and seen where I had come from. To go home now would mean wasting Pawpine's gold.

I headed south. Confident? Happy? Not on your life. As I shifted up through the gears I recalled a phrase from a novel, "It's gone south." The expression meant it's screwed up.

Under different conditions I would have enjoyed the drive down the Trace. It was a sunny day, the air was fresh after the storm, the scenery was pretty, and there were so few cars and campers on the road I could pretend it was mine.

But the closer I got to Natchez, the more real it all became and the deeper my nervousness grew. The Trace ended east of town at Highway 61, the same highway Mom had sung about in her most famous tune, and when I turned onto that road I did something I've done all my life, something I had practiced to perfection—I procrastinated.

On the edge of town was a strip of discount motels and fast-food restaurants. It was eight o'clock and I had driven all day. It wouldn't look good, I rationalized, to arrive late in the evening at my grandfather's house, dirty and underfed.

So I hit one of the greasy spoons on the strip and took away two jumbo hamburgers, a large order of fries, a fruit pie and a "maxi-jug" of ginger ale, then drove into a run-down motel called the Plantation Inn and parked under the sign that said Office/Vacancy in pink neon. The screen door creaked as I entered.

A moment later a middle-aged woman wearing a wrinkled apron pushed through a bead curtain and stood at the counter. Behind her a TV flickered—some game show or other—and I heard the muted cheers of the audience.

The woman crossed her pale arms on the countertop. "Help you?" she said, deadpan. A drop of sweat trickled across her temple.

"I'd like a room for the night, please. Nonsmoking."

She eyed me up and down with the enthusiasm of a rattlesnake, looked past me to the dented truck idling outside the door.

"We're full up tonight."

"Oh," I said. "But the sign says you have a vacancy."

"All the rooms is reserved."

"You have nothing left?"

"I don't think y'all'd be happy here," she said with

finality. "Y'all might could try The Oaks just down the road."

She turned and slipped through the curtain, the beads rattling as they came back together.

What the hell's with her? I wondered as I got into the truck. I turned around in the empty lot. Although I counted at least twenty doors in the motel, only three had cars parked in front.

At The Oaks I was told by the manager, "Got lotsa room, son. Pretty slow around here this week."

"That's funny," I said. "The Plantation Inn was full."

"All booked up, you mean?" he said, smiling and running a broad hand over his bare scalp. The stubble on his face was white against his coal black skin. "You ain't from around here, are you?"

I registered and paid him in cash.

Once inside the small room, which was paneled with imitation wood and smelled damp and musty, I activated the air conditioner, flicked on the TV, collapsed in the one armchair, and watched a ball game as I wolfed down my supper. With the food sitting in my stomach like a stone, I stripped down and took a long cool shower. Then I dressed in fresh clothes. I sat on the bed and picked up the phone.

First, I called Montreal. I tried to sound breezy and noncommittal as I answered the standard list of parent questions—the How-are-you? and Did-you-remember? variety. The blues festival was great, Dad told me. Mom was knocking them dead, getting standing ovations, making lots of contacts. He was practicing his

French, visiting art galleries and museums. Had my marks from school come in the mail yet? Mom wanted to know. Was I eating enough?

"No, and I'm still alive, Mom," I told her.

After I said good-bye I phoned my grandparents.

"What's with the phone company?" Grandpa complained. "You're not fixed yet?"

I assured him that the company had promised they'd be out tomorrow to check the lines.

"I'll bet," he said. "Heard from your mom and dad?"

I gave him a quick summary and promised to call again tomorrow.

I failed to find anything worth watching on any of the four channels, so I undressed and slid between the damp sheets. The rooms on each side of me were empty and quiet. The air conditioner whined and clunked, smothering most of the noise from the highway, charging the air with stale odor more than cooling it.

I couldn't sleep. Would I find my grandfather tomorrow? And if I did, how would he react to my springing up from nowhere without warning? What was the big secret that had come between my mother and him?

It had rained during the night, but not enough to clean the mud and dust from the Toyota, which looked forlorn and beaten under the late-morning sun. I tossed my bag into the cab, climbed into the truck, and removed the Christmas card from my front pocket and read the name and address written inside it for the hundredth time. I consulted my *Mississippi* road map, poring over the inset map of Natchez, and started the truck.

"Well, Grandpa," I said. "Here I come, ready or not."

St. Catherine Street was a tree-lined and canopied tunnel running between Pine and Cemetery Roads, flanked by grand old houses that favored white columns in front and galleries running down the sides. I parked in front of number 19 and walked up a flagstone path through a vast cloud of fragrant rose bushes. Gathering my resolve, I knocked on the big front door. My grandfather must be pretty well off, I mused.

The door opened to reveal an older woman, tall and straight as the columns on each side of her, wearing diamond stud earrings and a pink dress that set off her strawberry blond hair with white roots. Her thick eyebrows came together in a frown.

"Deliveries are made around the back," she said, her voice refined, her speech smooth and drawn out.

I had taken care that morning to wear clean pants and a white shirt. I hadn't thought I looked like a delivery boy.

"Excuse me, ma'am," I said in my politest tone, "I'm looking for Mr. Lucas Straight."

"Y'all have the wrong house," she said, stepping back and moving to close the door.

"But—" I drew the envelope from my shirt pocket. "This is 19 St. Catherine Street, isn't it?"

"Yes, it is. But no one of that name lives here, or ever has. Or ever would," she added with a withering frown. "I think you want the *other* St. Catherine Street, north of town. Now, if you'll excuse me."

And the door closed. So much for Southern hospitality.

The *other* St. Catherine Street was a dirt road running alongside a meandering river outside of town between Cemetery Road and the Mississippi River. This, I said to myself as I drove past a clapboard shack with two decrepit cannibalized cars in the front yard, is more like it. A plume of yellow dust followed the truck as I drove slowly, reading the faded names on mailboxes that stood on the roadside in front of frame bungalows spaced far enough apart to allow glimpses of the river through thick-trunked and moss-shrouded trees.

My stomach ached. I was finally here; I could feel it, and my courage melted in the baking sun and drifted away on the hot breeze that carried the odor of tepid water and rotting vegetation from the river. Why wasn't I excited, eager to shake my grandfather's hand? Because the Family Mystery would loom over our meeting like an unfinished fight. Because I had no idea whether my grandfather would embrace me or push me down the stairs. For the second time since I had arrived in Natchez, I procrastinated. Maybe I should just play it cool for a while, I thought, feel things out a little bit, before I let him know who I am.

The houses grew farther apart, the road bumpier and narrower. I followed a curve and was almost past the mailbox before I caught sight of the letters on it, . . . CAS STRAI . . ., which I took to be the remains of LUCAS STRAIGHT. I shut off the truck and let it coast to a stop on the shoulder.

The cabin was sided with weathered gray planks, its rusted tin roof shaded by those tall, wide-canopied trees I had seen many times in movies that take place in the South—live oaks. A veranda ran across the front and down one side of the house, and a picket fence that looked as if it hadn't seen paint since before I was born enclosed a hard-packed swept dirt yard. The place had an air of neatness and cleanliness. An old man sat in a chaise that hung on chains from the veranda rafters, fanning himself as he read a book.

Completely rattled by now, afraid to confront the stranger, I groped for a plan. I got out of the truck, opened the hood, and pulled the ignition wire out of the coil. I climbed into the cab, turned the key, and heard the motor turn over valiantly without firing. I got out again and stood in the dust of the road, shaking my head in mock frustration. I looked at the cabin.

The old man was watching me. I pushed open the front gate and walked across the yard. I stood in front of my grandfather.

It was him, all right. It had to be. His nose, sharply bridged and flared wide at the nostrils, was a double for my mother's, as was his high broad forehead. His thick upper lip was dented, like Louis Armstrong's.

I took off my hat, swallowed hard, and said, "Hi, sir, I—"

He put his book aside. "How are y'all doin' today?"

"Er, fine, thanks. And you?"

"Can't complain."

"I wonder if I could trouble you for a glass of water."

"Help yourself to a glass of tea, son."

I'm not even going to try to reproduce his accent. He spoke in a deep, raspy voice and dragged out his words, slipping in extra syllables, as if he had all day to complete a sentence.

There was a pitcher of amber liquid and a few empty plastic tumblers on a table beside the swing. A walking stick leaned against the house beside the table. When I had poured and tasted the iced tea he invited me to sit in the cane chair opposite him.

"Y'all want me to call a tow truck for you?"

"No! I mean, no, thanks, sir. I think I can get the truck going again."

"Y'all from up north somewheres, ain't you?"

"Ohio."

I picked that state because their license plates were blue and white, like Ontario's. I thought he might get suspicious if I told him the truth.

He nodded. "Thought so." The fan began to move again and the chains holding the swing creaked.

"Sure is hot down here," I commented. "And humid."

The old man nodded. The fan wafted back and forth.

"Do you live alone here?" I asked.

Another nod. "Got lots of relations nearby, though."

I couldn't think of anything else to say. I never have been good at small talk. So I set my empty glass on the table and stood up.

"Well, thanks for the tea. I guess I'll get to work on that truck."

"Give a yell if y'all need a hand," he said.

The afternoon sun threw shadows across the road. I lay on my back in the dirt and pulled myself under the truck and looked at the oily underside of the engine for a while, dragging out my little masquerade and wondering what to do next. I shifted my position so I could see the porch. He hadn't picked up his book. He was watching me. Maybe he's suspicious, I thought. A young guy from up north turns up in his front yard asking questions, no wonder he's wary.

I struggled out from under the Toyota, beat the dust off my pants, and leaned over the outside fender, peering at the little four-cylinder engine like a surgeon working up a diagnosis. When I looked up at the gallery the old man was smoking a pipe. A while later he stood, picked up the cane, and walked stiffly down the steps and through the gate.

He was taller than I had thought, thin and wiry, with a slight stoop. He leaned on the cane as he moved, as if his right knee was locked. Before he got to me I reseated the cable in the coil and straightened up.

"Think I found the problem," I said.

"Uh-huh."

"Would you believe it, a loose wire."

And I'm your grandson, I almost blurted. Instead I

got into the truck as he stood leaning on his cane and looking at the motor. I turned the key and the engine came to life. I revved it a bit for show.

Now what? I asked myself. Maybe I'll just take off home and write him a letter. I had dug myself into a hole by pretending and I felt stupid, conscious that, if I revealed my identity now, he would probably think I belonged in a mental home. I sat there, furious at myself for being a coward but not angry enough to rouse my courage.

Instead I said, "Sir, do you mind if I ask your name?"

"Lucas Straight," he said. He paused, and when I said nothing he added, "And yours?"

This was my chance. If I told him, what would he do? Tell me to take a hike? Scream curses? Like so many other times in my life I sat mute, my brain in neutral. I took a deep breath. "Mike Wilkes," I said, using Jen's last name.

"Well, Mike," he rasped around the stem of his pipe, "y'all seem right handy with motors."

"I . . .well . . . I took auto shop at school."

"Up there in Ohio." He pronounced it *Oh-high-uh.*

"Yeah."

"Tell you what, Mike. I got a old pump over yonder in the shed, don't run at all. I use it to pump water up from the bayou when the well's low. If you could get it goin' again, I'd be glad to pay you for your trouble."

I almost jumped out of the truck. "Sure."

"Park in the driveway, then. They's tools in the shed, you need any."

And with that he turned and walked to the veranda.

Behind the house, the yard was shaded by live oaks trailing gray scarves of Spanish moss. A jetty jutted into the still, caramel-colored water of the bayou, and a lawn chair was tied to one of the pilings with a length of frayed plastic rope. On the opposite shore was a cypress swamp, its skeletal trunks rising into the hard blue sky and striping the water with shadows.

The pump motor, an old four-stroke, hadn't seen a wrench in a long time. The oil in the sump was black with age. The gas tank was full. I pulled the starter a few times and got no response, not even a cough. I lifted the pump onto the wide, waist-high shelf built into the side of the shed, then looked inside the shed for the tools. The spark plug was so fouled it would never fire again. The carburetor parts were varnished from sitting inactive for a long time, so I cleaned them with a brush and steel wool.

Working on the pump relaxed me somewhat. When I had reinstalled the carb I stood and stretched. It was then that I noticed the mud-smeared license plate on the front of the truck and remembered that in most states cars carried plates only on the rear bumper.

I sneaked a glance at the house, then quickly removed the plate, skinning my knuckles in my haste, and tossed it under the seat. Then I scooped a gob of grease from the plastic container I had seen in the shed and smeared it over the word *Ontario* on the rear plate. And not a second too soon. I heard a screen door creak open and slap shut. My grandfather limped over to my work place, a glass of tea in his hand.

"Thought you might like something," he offered.

"Thanks, Mr. Straight."

"Call me Lucas, Mike."

"Um, okay." I held up the spark plug from the pump. "If you can tell me where to go, I'll pick up a new one for you. This one's shot."

Lucas gave me directions to a garage on the edge of town. "Don't go to the Texaco," he stressed. "White man owns that one."

I got there just as they were closing and bought the plug. Back at the house, I installed it, and on the second pull of the starter cord the motor fired and purred away like new. I let it run for half a minute and shut it off—without water flowing through it the pump mechanism would overheat. Then I disassembled the pump, cleaned it up, greased the parts, and put them back together.

By the time I finished, night had begun to fall and the lights were on in the house. I cleaned my hands on a rag and knocked on the front door.

"Come on back into the kitchen, Mike," I heard.

I stood there for a few moments, savoring the odors of pipe smoke and cooking meat—I was hungry—until I remembered that *I* was Mike. The door opened into a small parlor with a fireplace and a couch and chair with tattered upholstery. Passing through, I noticed his book, *Panthers in Chains*, on an end table and faded photos of Martin Luther King Jr. and Malcolm X on the wall.

The kitchen was at the back of the house, and it wasn't exactly a contender for a home-and-gardens magazine. There was a single tap over the sink, a two-burner propane stove, a few cupboards. On a small round table two places had been set.

"Y'all can wash up at the sink yonder," Lucas said, putting a platter of fried chicken on the table. "Supper's ready."

I was ready too. The fried chicken, bread and butter, and iced tea were followed by raisin oatmeal cookies right out of the bag. We didn't talk much as we ate—which was a relief to me since I didn't have to think up a bunch of lies while I munched.

"Guess you'll be movin' on tomorrow," Lucas said, settling back into his chair and wiping crumbs from his mouth with the back of his hand.

"Yeah."

I knew he was waiting for me to tell him where I was headed. I had realized by then that he thought it was bad manners to ask a lot of questions. I said no more. I nibbled on a cookie instead, putting off the moment when I'd have to leave.

Lucas reached into his pocket and laid a ten-dollar bill on the table.

"'Preciate your help with that pump," he said.

"No, that's all right, Mr.—Lucas. I was glad to do it."

"Mike, I asked for your help. Don't let's talk no more about it."

"Okay. Thanks." I took up the money.

"Where you plannin' to spend the night?"

"The truck's rigged for camping. I'll find a spot somewhere."

"Y'all're welcome to camp right out there in the driveway if you want."

"Okay," I said, hoping my relief didn't show. "Thanks."

I bedded down in the truck, my stomach full, my head ringing with thoughts and questions. In a way I was satisfied now. I had met my grandfather. He seemed like an okay guy. And now that he was a real person to me rather than a distant abstraction I felt more confident. Tomorrow I would tell him who I was. If he threw me out, I'd go home without regret. But not until I found out what had happened between him and my mother, although I was beginning to have an idea. I had a right to know for sure. I was his grandson. He owed it to me.

I slept fitfully, tossing and turning in the heat, until a sharp noise down by the river woke me. The damp, sticky air was dead still, heavy with ripe odors from the bayou. Straining to hear more, I caught only the *chirrup* of crickets, *galump* of frogs, and the hum of insects. The memory of the cops' attack pushed into my mind, setting my nerves on edge. Leaning on my elbow, I craned my neck to see out the front of the truck.

Down at the jetty, a strong light was trained on the water. A shadow passed in front of it.

My heart began to pound and my breath came faster. I willed my eyes to see more and failed—the sky was a black dome without moon or stars. Momentarily, something blocked the light again and I heard a faint splash.

I pushed my sleeping bag away and climbed through the narrow window into the cab, feeling for the keys in the ignition. If I had to, I could start the truck and get out of there within seconds. I sat behind the wheel in my underwear, eyes fixed on the light. Who was on the jetty? What was he doing there in the middle of the night? Had he come from the bayou to burgle Lucas's house, knowing only an old man lived there?

The figure moved again. He had something long and slender in his hand.

A rifle.

The invader bent over, stood, bent again. Another splash. Now fully awake, my brain began to function. I had to warn my grandfather. I put my hand on the door handle, let go, letting out a long breath. I had almost made a mistake. I reached up and flicked the switch on the cab light so it wouldn't come on when the door was opened.

Moving in slow motion, I slipped out of the truck, letting the door hang open. The ground was cool and wet on my bare feet. I crept through the dark, along the side of the shed, my fingers gliding over the rough planks to guide me. I crouched behind a tree, held my breath, and watched the figure on the jetty.

And I felt a fire of anger working its way into my limbs. Who did that jerk think he was, sneaking onto my grandfather's land with a gun in his hand? A desperate plan formed in my mind.

I slipped back to the truck, reached inside and switched on the headlights.

In the white glare of the truck's high beams, on the end of the jetty, a man rose and turned my way in one jerky motion, throwing one arm up before his eyes. As if in a photograph I saw that in his other hand he held a fishing rod. Beside him, next to the lawn chair, was a white plastic bucket. A second fishing rod leaned against a piling, the line curving gently from the tip to a bobber in the center of the pool of light on the water.

It was Lucas.

"What the—" he exclaimed as he took a step backward, hitting the chair with his game leg, and toppled off the jetty, uttering a cry as a fountain of water rushed up into the glare.

I began to run. "I'm sorry! I'm sorry!" I shouted as my feet pounded on the jetty. I jumped off the end into the warm chest-deep water. My feet sank into mud that squished obscenely between my toes. Frantically I reached to grab Lucas and was rewarded with a clout in the eye from his thrashing arms. Unable to get his feet under him, he beat the water uselessly, throwing up a confusion of foam and muddy water.

Wading behind him, I wrapped my arms around his chest and dragged him onto the slippery bank.

"What in the name of all that's holy d'y'all think you're doing?" he thundered, spluttering and sitting up. His voice, carried on the damp night air, echoed back from the far side of the bayou.

"I heard a noise. I thought I saw someone with a gun."

Lucas wiped his face and spat river water onto the ground. "A gun? Y'all seen too many movies, boy. Now, go on back in the drink and fetch my pole!"

I waded into the bayou, grabbed the float, and pulled on the line, hand over hand, until the fishing rod rose to the surface. I tossed it onto the jetty and waded to shore, shivering with disgust at the sucking mud around my feet.

Lucas stood dripping in the harsh light, his sopping shirt and overalls clinging to his bony frame. When he saw me scrabble onto the bank in my underwear he began to laugh.

"What's so damn funny?" I said, though it wasn't him I was angry at.

"Mike," he chortled, "y'all look like a bull catfish done had a bad night!"

He threw back his head and his laughter echoed across the bayou once more.

"I'm sorry," I said lamely for a third time. "Are you all right?"

"Turn off them darned lights," he rasped, "and let's go inside and get dry."

Later, we sat on the jetty in the tranquil darkness, a vacuum jug of hot coffee between our chairs, two red-and-white bobbers floating in the light on the still water. Three small crappies and two catfish bumped their noses against the sides of the white bucket and worked their gills.

"You know," Lucas said slowly, "when I was a boy the swamp and bush over yonder was full of fish and wild game."

"Were there panthers?"

He chuckled as he threaded a fresh wriggling minnow on his hook. "Panthers? In Mississippi? Where'd you get such an idea?"

"I saw your book."

Lucas laughed again. I was beginning to feel like the straight man in a comedy duo.

"That's a history of the Black Panthers," he told me, casting his line. "They was a militant Black Power outfit back in the sixties. Done a lot of good too, even though some of 'em preached armed rebellion. The system done 'em in, though, like it always does."

He slapped a mosquito on the back of his neck. "How's that eye of yours?"

Gingerly, I touched the pulpy flesh under the prize-winning shiner that half closed my eye. "It's all right. Maybe it'll make me look tough."

Lucas laughed. "It will that," he said. "It will that. Hey! Y'all got a bite."

We fished all night, sitting quietly together, listening to the night sounds of the swamp and watching the stars appear when a breeze came up to clear off the clouds. In the morning we returned to the house and washed up.

"Y'all grab some sleep in the spare room," Lucas said, hoisting the pail of fish onto the counter beside the sink.

I dragged myself into the small bedroom beside his and without turning on the light, kicked off my shoes, lay down and fell into a dreamless sleep.

When I padded into the kitchen the next morning, yawning and knuckling the sleep from my eyes—and yelping when I mashed the tender flesh of my shiner—Lucas was pouring coffee. On the table were two plates, each bearing a sandwich made with thick slices of white bread.

Clean-shaven, and dressed in black trousers and a long-sleeved white shirt with a black tie, Lucas looked unlike the fisherman of last night. A suit jacket hung on the back of one of the chairs.

"Mornin', Mike. Sit down and dig in."

Hungry from staying up all night, a bit bleary-eyed with fatigue, I took a bite of my sandwich. Whatever was between the bread was warm, crispy, and delicious. I finished in four or five bites and drained my mug.

"How's the eye?" Lucas asked, a tinge of embarrassment in his voice.

"A bit better. The swelling's gone down a bit."

Lucas nodded.

"That sandwich was good," I said. "What was it?"

"Fried catfish. More coffee?"

"Er, sure." The image of one of those ugly flat-headed and whiskered creatures with the black eel-like body slithered into my mind. I was glad I had asked him after the meal.

"One of the ones we hauled in last night. The rest of our catch is in the freezer."

Lucas set my refilled cup on the table. "Mike, I hope you'll forgive my bein' rude, but, are you plannin' to move on today?"

I had been looking out the window across the yard to the gold sunlight on the bayou, and his question caught me by surprise. Leaving that peaceful place was the last thing in my mind.

"Um, yeah. I guess so," I stammered.

"Reason I ask," he continued. "I got to go to a funeral today. I should phone my nephew soon. He'll carry me to the church in his car."

I felt hurt. My own grandfather was rushing me out the door. Okay, I was being stupid. I knew that. To Lucas I was a stranger named Mike from up north, who he'd known for a day. But we had spent the whole night fishing together, him telling me stories about the places and people around Natchez, his quiet voice and our laughter drifting like smoke into the inky darkness. He had shown me how to bait a hook with a worm or minnow—which he pronounced *minner*—and how to tell the difference between a crappie's anxious strike at the bait and the cagey tug of a catfish. Now it was over.

"It's okay, Mr. Straight," I assured him. "I understand. I was planning to— Hey! Wait a minute. Why not let me take you to the funeral? I'd be glad to. I'll drop you off and leave from there."

"Well, I don't want to put you to no trouble."

Half an hour later, showered and wearing my last set of clean, not-too-wrinkled clothes, I drove along a series of dirt roads through flat green fields. Lucas sat beside me, his polished shoes resting on a carpet of fast-food wrappers, his cane between his knees.

"Was the— Is the funeral for a relative?" I asked him.

"A good friend," he answered solemnly. "A real good friend."

"I'm sorry."

"Oh, it was a blessing when he passed. A release. Poor ol' Ray had the cancer, smoked like a fiend all his life, two or three packs a day. He had a lot of pain at the end. Take the next left, Mike. That's the church over yonder."

I brought the truck to a stop where a gaggle of pick-ups and older sedans huddled in the shade of an oak. A hearse and two black cars were parked by the church steps.

"Ain't been to a service since the last funeral I went to," he said.

"You're not religious, eh?" I asked, mentally slapping myself for the Canadianism. I'd been successful so far, I thought, in keeping "eh?" from my speech for fear I'd give myself away.

But Lucas seemed not to notice. "No, I ain't. Christianity was imposed on us by the white man when our ancestors came here from Africa. It was a means of keepin' us down, encouragin' us to accept things the way they were. I was raised a Baptist but I threw it off when I was a teenager, when I learned how the world worked and got my mind straight. But this is neither the time nor the place," he went on. "You're welcome to come on in, Mike."

"No, sir, thanks. I guess I'll say good-bye here."

"Well, don't say it yet. There's a picnic after the service. I'd like you to come, 'less you're in a hurry."

"No. No, I'm not."

"Good." He closed the door and limped toward the church.

I had decided while I drove not to tell Lucas who I really was. It would be a dirty trick to drop such a bomb on him on his way to his friend's funeral. No, I'd write to him when I got home, thank him for his hospitality, hope he wrote back. As for the Family Mystery, well, I could ask him in my letter.

I had noticed a phone booth at a gas station we had passed, and after Lucas disappeared into the shadow of the church door I drove there, prepared to commit fraud against my parents and grandparents again. Luckily, Mom and Dad weren't in their hotel room. "See you in a few days," I chirped to the answering service. My grandparents weren't home, so I left a message there too.

I pulled the truck in alongside the pumps, got out, and began to fill the tank. It was hot. It was hotter than hot. The still air smelled of gasoline and oily dust and coffee from the convenience store attached to the gas bar. There was little traffic in this part of town. I was trying to decide if the community was as dull as Fergus when a big pickup, shiny and blue and wet from a car wash, roared up to the pumps, clouds of dust pluming from the wheels. Country music twanged and moaned from the cab, and in the rear window hung a Confederate flag. The passenger, a long-haired man in a faded baseball hat, threw me a malevolent stare. Behind his head a pump shotgun lay cradled in a wooden rack.

The driver's door slammed and a denim-clad middle-aged man appeared from behind the truck, unscrewed the gas cap, and slammed the pump nozzle into the opening. He peered at me from under the bill of his cap, then scanned my truck, his pale blue eyes lingering on the license plate. There was a black line under his lower lip, as if he'd put mascara on the wrong place, but the effect was more sinister than comic.

"How's ever' little thing up north?" he sneered, his accent as thick as glue, then he leaned forward a bit and spat out a long stream of tobacco juice. The dark liquid rolled in the dust like a gob of motor oil.

"Fine, thanks," I said evenly.

I felt scorn and fear at the same time. This was a cliché if I had ever seen one—the truck, the music, the flag and gun and tobacco juice, the unconcealed contempt for a black kid in a beat-up Toyota. I wondered if the two louts wore tattoos under their shirts, read right-wing outdoors magazines, slunk home each day to mobile homes where overweight women named Bobbie-Jo or Wendy-Lou poured a Bud for them before target practice.

I pulled the nozzle from the tank inlet and replaced

the gas cap, knowing I had only taken on a couple of gallons. I wanted out of there, fast.

"Ain't they got no American trucks up there?"

"Um, my dad couldn't afford one," I said lamely, hoping my voice didn't shake as much as it seemed to me.

"Strange," the man in the truck drawled over the guitars and banjos, "your kind gettin' all the good jobs nowadays." His voice was heavy with menace. "Or collectin' welfare all yer life."

Ignoring the impulse to make a snide comment about the contradiction, I turned my back and walked to the store. Hands trembling, I handed over the money.

"Y'all come on back, now," said the teenage clerk, smiling and popping her gum as she stuffed the bills into the cash register.

Maybe not, I thought as I pulled out of the lot. I turned on the windshield washers to clean the smear of tobacco juice from the glass.

Back at the church, I parked under the same tree, grateful for the breeze that sighed in the branches overhead, rustling the leaves and flowing into the cab. In the small white building the singing had started, loud, harmonious and joyful—not at all what I'd have expected at a funeral.

The aftereffect of the adrenaline rush from the scene at the gas station left my muscles soft and quivering, and I felt the full weight of my black skin. More than once in my life I had secretly wished that I wasn't half-African, and guilt had always followed, as if I was betraying my mother. After reading about Pawpine I had begun to be proud, a little at first, that I was connected to the generations of women and children and men who as slaves had built the farms and plantations of the South and then had migrated north and west to build airplanes, trucks, machines, and roads. Now I was reminded that there was nowhere to hide.

The music faded and died in the church, replaced by birdsong. A few moments later a procession flowed from the church door and down the steps, the coffin floating like a leaf on the stream of mourners. In the graveyard the burial proceeded at a leisurely pace. White handkerchiefs flashed in the sun, were raised and lowered.

After pausing to speak to a few people, Lucas limped slowly toward me. Behind him the small crowd broke up and drifted toward the cars. I got out and opened the door for him, then came around and climbed in again. Lucas sat for a moment without speaking. Around us, car motors came to life and the mourners drove away.

"Well, that's that," Lucas murmured. "Ol' Ray's in the ground. Let's go, Mike."

The picnic was held at Ray's widow's house, a place much like Lucas's, on a back road near the Mississippi River, but with a much bigger yard. Mrs. James sat on a rocking chair on the veranda, greeting her guests as they arrived. Lucas spoke to her for a few moments, then called me up to meet her.

She was a large, capable-looking woman, formal in her black dress, and her handshake was firm. "Y'all are welcome to our home, Mike," she said.

Inwardly I winced at hearing my phony name. "Thank you for having me, Mrs. James." I said.

"Go on down there, you two, and get somethin' to eat."

Beside the frame house a trestle table sagged under the weight of enough food to feed the two dozen or so assembled people several times over—platters of chicken fried golden brown, huge bowls of creamy potato salad and coleslaw, dishes of rice and beans, cakes, pies and tarts galore, and a long metal tray of shredded meat that gave off a tangy mouth-watering aroma. Tubs of crushed ice at each end of the table held beer and soda.

"What's that?" I asked Lucas, pointing to the meat.

"Why, that's barbecue," he said. "Get you some. Can't go back to Oh-high-uh without tryin' real barbecue."

With our plates stacked high we found chairs in the shade and began to eat. Little white butterflies danced in the long grass around us, and farther away a few kids played catch. It was the first time in my life I had been to a social function of any kind where everybody was black. People stood or sat around the veranda, the men jacketless, with their sleeves rolled up past their elbows. The women had removed their hats and fanned themselves with their hankies as they talked and ate. Whenever someone passed by us, Lucas would introduce me. I got lots of exercise standing up and sitting, and saw lots of smiles when Lucas explained my shiner. He obviously enjoyed telling the story, and each time he did, there was a little more detail, a fraction more drama.

"Yonder's my two nephews," Lucas said, pointing with his chin at two long-legged, athletic-looking men about Dad's age. "Ned and Cal. Cal's the one with the bad arm."

The taller man's left arm was shorter than his right and it hung uselessly at his side, twisted so that the back of his hand touched the side of his leg.

"And them's their wives, Rose and Sharon," Lucas added as he wiped his plate clean with the last of a bread roll.

Sharon was the widest woman I had ever seen. Her huge buttocks rose and fell like pistons as she walked. Rose was big too, but her sister-in-law made her look almost slender. Carrying two plates of food each, they joined their husbands.

I watched my mother's cousins. Cal leaned close to Rose and whispered in her ear. Frowning fiercely, she elbowed him, knocking his fork from his hand and sending a gob of potato salad down the front of his shirt. Sharon let out a laugh, then clapped her palm over her mouth. Ned smiled, shaking his head like a schoolteacher.

"What happened to Cal's arm?" I asked Lucas.

He gnawed the last shred of meat from a chicken bone and dropped it on his plate. When he spoke there was a hard edge to his voice. "When Cal and Ned were younger than you, 'round twelve, I guess, they was real hellions. Got mixed up in the civil rights movement. Back there in the sixties. At Selma, Cal managed to get hisself in the first row of a demonstration. A police dog got at him. Chewed his arm up real bad before the cop got it under control. Probably wasn't in much of a hurry, the cop. Cal almost bled to death."

"It's hard to believe they used dogs on people, isn't it?"

"Yep. And fire hoses, and nightsticks. That was in the daytime, in front of the TV cameras and reporters. After dark, some people used guns and even bombs. You probably learned about this in school."

"Yeah, some." The American civil rights movement wasn't exactly a big item back in Canada, especially in Fergus.

"Well, that was a bad time," he went on, shaking his

head. "Between the movement and the war, a lot of blood flowed. A lot of boys from around here never made it to thirty."

Lucas put his empty plate down on the grass and drained his tea. I had finished eating. I said nothing, unwilling to interrupt the flow of his thought.

"Fought our war here against the white man's laws—Mississippi was the worst state in the union to live in if you was black—and fought the white man's war over there in Vietnam. Lost both of 'em."

Lucas drew his pipe from a shirt pocket and a tobacco pouch from his trousers. He began to fill the pipe. Most of the picnickers had finished eating and a few women and men moved among them, collecting paper plates on trays. My mother's cousins were playing cards, Cal dealing one-handed.

As Lucas lit his pipe with a wooden match, I asked him, "Did Cal and Ned fight in the war? The one in Vietnam, I mean."

"No, they was too young."

"Did you?"

Lucas took his pipe from his mouth and spat into the grass. "Nope. I was drafted around the time they were shutting the war down, but I refused to go. You know, Ray and me, we knew each other all our lives. That's the onliest thing we ever really argued about. He said we ought to fight for our country. I said I wouldn't go to some little place in Asia and shoot people I had no quarrel with. No coincidence those Asian people wasn't white, Mike. None at all."

He let out a laugh, thin and bitter as vinegar. "No

freedom here in Mississippi, not if you was black. White man kept us down here—still does—and at the same time sent us to fight for freedom, as they put it, in 'Nam. Well, not Lucas Straight. I went to jail instead. That's where I hurt my leg, broke it real bad on a work gang. Not that I was against a shooting war for the right reasons. If we'd been fightin' the white man for instance. Yeah, whites is bastards, Mike, ever' damn one of 'em.

"But," he said with a wave of his hand that made it clear he was done with the subject, "that was ages ago, and this ain't the time or place to talk about it. If you don't mind, I'd like some more tea. Sure is hot today."

With my lunch turning sour in my stomach, I took Lucas's glass to the trestle table, which now looked as if it had been carpet bombed. The platters were bare, the bowls scraped clean. I found a sweating pitcher of tea and filled the glass.

I'm not sure when it had dawned on me, but by the time Lucas had stopped talking I realized, after knowing him only a day and a half, that I had found the answer to the Family Mystery.

My grandfather hated whites, and my mother had married one.

The afternoon wore on, shadows inched their way across the yard, a few whisky bottles appeared and someone called for music. Moments later Cal, Ned, and another man along with a tall, good-looking woman whose gold earrings reminded me of Mom's were sitting in kitchen chairs on the veranda. Cal held a harmonica, Ned unpacked a banjo, the other two tuned acoustic guitars, and soon music as familiar to me as my name filled the hot summer air—classic blues.

On some of the tunes the guests added their voices to the lonesome wail of the harmonica. Ned's fingers blurred on the banjo strings. The guitar players were almost as good. Even Lucas added his rich, gravelly bass—he could sing harmony effortlessly, it seemed. I mumbled along when I recognized a song, but my heart wasn't in it. I was lost in thought.

If I'd had any brains, or if I had considered the matter for any length of time, I guess I could have figured out the Family Mystery myself, and to an outsider it probably seems strange that I didn't. Family disagreements and breakups happened all the time, for all sorts of reasons. But having a black mother and a white father, having no experience of Mom's side of the family, had always been a fact of life for me. Besides, it would never have occurred to me that someone wouldn't like my father. Everybody liked him. And why shouldn't they? He was a terrific guy.

But my grandfather, I knew now, had hated him enough to cut his own daughter loose for good. As far as Lucas Straight was concerned, Etta had gone over to the enemy, and the man who had been strong willed enough to go to jail rather than fight in a hypocritical war had disowned her.

The foursome on the gallery had stopped singing and now people were taking turns naming a tune, standing, and singing solo until the others scattered in the grass around them joined in.

I decided that telling Lucas my identity was a dead issue. I'd never see him again. I wasn't sure I wanted to. I had blamed Mom for cutting me off from my African roots, but I knew the truth now. I'd get an early start in the morning and close the book on Lucas Straight.

"Mike!" a voice boomed from across the yard. "Your turn, son!"

"And don't try to use that shiner as an excuse," Sharon said with a laugh. "Y'all got to sing for your lunch!"

In my neck and face I felt the familiar hot flush that came when I was centered out, and I wished I could have slunk away through the grass.

"Come on, Mike," Lucas said. A smile lit his face and crinkled the skin at the corners of his eyes. "Give us a song."

All right, you bigoted old man, I thought bitterly, I'll give you a song.

I got to my feet, my anger chasing away embarrassment. I scanned the faces turned expectantly toward me. Some of these people were related to me, and the man beside me had kept me from them.

"Um, I don't know if any of you have heard this one," I faltered, clearing the sand from my throat, my mind racing over the lines. I turned to face Lucas. "It's called 'South on 61.' My mother wrote it."

Lucas nodded and leaned on the cane between his knees. I tried to remember the things Mom had taught me about singing in public—not that I had ever expected to—how to breathe, to squeeze the words up from my diaphragm, and for a moment I wished I had taken music lessons as she had urged me many times. Under my breath I hummed for a second to get the starting note. Then I began.

Well, I'm headin' south on 61,
I'm goin' home again,
Back to where I came from,
Back to all the pain.
My leavin' was so desperate,
My comin' home's the same.

Cotton broke my daddy's back
It broke his daddy's too,
But Chicago's long assembly lines
Are silent as a tomb.
They drove him back down 61
With nothin' but the blues.

The woman with the guitar began chording along with me and Ned had picked out the harmony on his banjo. The second guitar had come in on the fourth line of stanza two, adding a rich counterpoint to the banjo. Cal waited until the beginning of stanza three, then laid down a sad faraway shading with the harmonica.

Oh, Mama, why'd you leave me?
Why you been gone so long?
It's now that I most need you
To say where I belong.
I'm headin' back down 61
With nothin' but this song.

Ol' 61, she led us north
To jobs, prosperity,
And gave us frozen ghettos
And a life of misery.
She runs in two directions,
And neither one is free.

I'm headin' back down 61,
I'm goin' home again.
My leavin' was so desperate,
My comin' home's the same.

It was long past dark when I parked the truck in Lucas's driveway. As soon as the motor died the night noises leaped from the clammy dark, and the moon threw a broad silver stripe across the bayou and dappled the front yard with soft blue light.

All the way home he had raved about the song and complimented me on my singing. I had made polite sounds, but made it clear to him I didn't feel like talking.

"Better let me go first," Lucas said, "and put the light on."

Inside, he struggled out of his suit jacket and hung it on a kitchen chair. "I'm gonna heat me up some milk and take it to bed," he said. "Want some?"

"No, thanks, Mr. Straight."

"Helps me sleep," he added, taking a pot down from a cupboard. He splashed some milk into the pot and turned on the burner. "I ain't gonna fish tonight, but you're welcome to try your luck."

Knowing I wouldn't be able to sleep for hours, I took him up on his offer.

"Sure," he said enthusiastically. "They don't usually bite so good when the moon's on the water, but you never know." He turned off the burner and poured the milk into a mug. "Switch for the night-light is right there on the jetty. You know where the tackle is. Should be lots of minners left in the tank."

"Okay, great."

"Well, good night, Mike."

"'Night, Mr. Straight. Um, I'll probably take off early tomorrow, so please don't trouble yourself over making breakfast for me."

"Well, least I can do," he said, "for a famous blues singer, is make some coffee." He smiled. "And for an old fishin' buddy."

He hobbled down the hall and went into his room.

I set out two fishing lines and sat in the lawn chair at the end of the jetty in a world of sound—the croak and *kerchunk* of frogs, the cheep of crickets, the whine of mosquitoes. A breeze swept up the bayou, wrinkling the water and bobbing the floats.

I was trying hard to dislike my grandfather, without much success. He seemed like a nice man, loyal to his friends, kind to a stranger, but his hatred of white people ran deep and his rejection of my mother and father wasn't something I could accept—or forgive. How could such powerful hatred and such easy kindness live together inside the same man?

I fished for a long time after the moon slid away. I caught a few crappies, but I tossed them back. I was damned if I'd save them for him.

I woke up at eight, pulled on my clothes, and padded down the hall to the kitchen. A pot of coffee simmered on the stove. Lucas was nowhere to be seen.

Good, I thought. I returned to the bedroom and made the bed and packed up my gear. Before I left the house for the last time I laid the copy of my Pawpine research paper beside Lucas's book on a table in the living room. I had brought it in from the truck the night before. Then I hoisted my pack onto my shoulder. The screen door slapped shut behind me.

Wearing a stained tank top, baggy jeans, and rubber boots, Lucas stood beside the Toyota with a hose in one hand and a big sponge in the other. The side of the truck gleamed in the morning sunlight, washed clean of mud and dust. He turned, nodded, and moved around to the tailgate, playing the stream against the truck, wiping with the sponge, rinsing off the dirt.

I opened the driver's door and tossed my gear into the cab. My vacuum bottle lay on the seat. I took off the cap, releasing the odor of hot coffee.

"Thanks for the coffee," I said grudgingly as I stepped to the back of the truck.

Lucas stood rooted to the spot, hands at his sides, the hose pouring unnoticed onto the toe of his boot. He stared at the clean white license plate with the blue letters and numbers and the word *Ontario* across the top.

"Dammit!" I whispered.

He looked up at me. Jaw muscles worked under his skin.

His whisper rasped like a file. "Who are you?"

It was over. I took a deep breath.

"My name is Zachariah Lane," I told him. "I'm your grandson."

His eyes saucered momentarily, then a frown creased his sweating forehead. His chin trembled and he turned his head to look out over the bayou. He swallowed.

"I didn't know Etta had no boy," he murmured. His gaze dropped to the wet ground at his feet. "Zachariah. That was my daddy's name. I didn't know I had a grandson."

"You don't," I said.

My words struck him like a blow, and his shoulders flinched. Without uttering another sound, he dropped the sponge and the hose and hobbled slowly and stiffly to the house. Without looking back, he went inside.

I shut off the hose, climbed into the truck, and drove away.

In planning my trip, I had thought about taking Highway 61 to Memphis on my way home, just so I could tell Mom I had done it, but things had changed. All I wanted to do now was point the truck north and get to Fergus as directly as possible. So, after stopping to replace the front license plate just outside Natchez, I took the Trace—not the fastest route, but it was familiar. At Nashville I got onto the Interstate and stayed on the big highways. The trip home was depressing and long, and it was dark when I pulled into our driveway a couple of days later.

I was exhausted, as depleted as an empty sack, but I still had my wits about me. The first thing I did was erase my phony message from our answering machine and then call my parents in Montreal. Mom sounded as tired as I felt, said she was anxious to get home. I curbed my urge to tell her where I'd been, to tell her I was sorry for misjudging her for so long, because to do so would have upset her. I hung up, promising myself I'd find a way to make it up to her.

I called my grandparents and, as cheerfully as I could, announced that the telephone had been fixed.

"About time," Grandpa said.

It felt good to be home. I made my way through the house, turning on a light in every room, and each time I did I was greeted by withering plants drooping accusingly in their pots. I threw open a few widows to clear out the stale air, then made a dozen trips to and from the plants with Mom's favorite hammered-brass watering can.

I collected my gear from the truck, wincing at the sight of the crumpled fender and hood, and threw all my clothes into the washing machine before taking a hot shower. I put on a pair of boxers and a tank top, slipped into my flip-flops, and walked out to the road to collect the mail. I tossed the junk mail into the recycling box and piled the rest on the table inside the front door. The stack of envelopes reminded me that my report card should be arriving soon. I had done my best to salvage my credits and I was pretty sure that, although my marks wouldn't make my parents glow with pride and rush out to buy me a new car, I had passed everything.

Except, maybe, history. That depended on how Ms. Song had liked my Pawpine essay.

Even if she had given me the credit, university acceptance was touch and go. I had applied to three places and hadn't received early acceptance from any of them. It had been a rough two weeks in June when other kids got theirs, strutting around and pretending to be surprised, babbling excitedly about courses and residence fees, clubs and teams. I'd have to wait until the end of the summer. Wait and hope.

I popped open a can of tonic water and, in my room,

took Pawpine's white straps and neck iron out of my dresser drawer and looked at them. I wished I still had his gold, but it had probably been melted down by now. I wondered what the jeweler had made from it—a ring, maybe, or the setting for a precious stone in a pendant or brooch. Maybe some woman was wearing it right now, the gold with all that history resting against unknowing white skin at a boring party in a boring town. Well, it was none of my business anymore.

In each hand I held a strap, overcome once again by pity and admiration and affection for the man who had lived his days in an alien world against his will. Pawpine's life had given me the inspiration to go south and find my roots. His gold had given me the means. No matter what kind of hell I caught from my parents, I would never be sorry.

I knew now why Mom had stayed distant from her family. And I knew I had blamed the wrong person. My mother and father lived for each other. Even though they were my parents, I knew their love was like gold, and Lucas's hate was like the silt that clogged the bayou behind his house. My mother would never accept someone who hated my father, not even her own father. She had been forced to make a choice, and being with my grandfather even for a short time had given me a whisper of an idea how hard it must have been for her.

I picked up Pawpine's neck iron. To be hated, I thought, to be exiled from your home, must be the worst thing in the world.

PART FOUR

As soon as the clock on our mantel chimed nine o'clock I picked up the phone. On the eighth ring a grumpy voice came on.

"Piffard's Jewelry."

I had awakened in the middle of the night to the sigh of a gentle rain, and as I slipped through the dark rooms closing windows an idea had formed in my groggy head: Maybe Mr. Piffard hadn't sold Pawpine's gold. Maybe I could buy it back.

In the morning I fretted and paced from the time I got up until the main street stores opened.

"Um, Mr. Piffard," I began.

"This is he."

"It's Zack Lane calling."

"Oh, yes."

He said it the way people do when they don't have a clue who you are but don't want to admit it.

"I sold . . . You bought a gold nugget from me a while ago."

"Oh, that. Yes, I remember," he said warily.

"Well, I was just wondering if you still have it."

"Why?"

I hated it when people answered a question with

another question. Why was Piffard being cagey? You'd have thought I was accusing him of peddling Rolex knockoffs.

"Because I want to know," I answered, as politely as I could.

"Well, I don't have it."

"I see," I said. "Can you tell me where it is?"

"That's really not possible."

"No, I mean, did you melt it down, make something out of it? Or is it still in its original condition?"

I paused, desperate to hear him tell me that the nugget was whole and sound, waiting for me somewhere. I hurried on. "Because if it is, maybe I could buy it back from whoever has it now."

"It's gone. I'm afraid that's all I can say."

"But—"

"Good morning." And he hung up.

"You scum," I muttered, slamming down the phone.

I was worse off than I had been before I called. If Piffard had told me he had made a brooch out of the gold, I could have handled that. But to think the nugget might still exist, that if I only knew whoever had bought it I could make them an offer, drove me batty.

Vowing never again to follow half-baked ideas that came to me in the middle of the night, I pushed through the kitchen door, pulled the lawn mower and trimmer out of the garage, and spent the morning vengefully attacking the grass, seeing Piffard's squinty eyes and smelly cigar stub in every blade.

After a shower and a lunch of "the yellow death," I

brought in the mail. Among the envelopes I found one from my school. It was addressed to Mr. and Mrs., but I told myself it was my report card inside and opened it anyway, a little surprised at how calm I was as I unfolded the computer-generated document whose lines and squares, course codes, averages, and medians and, in bold print down the right side, final grades, would tell me my future.

"Hooray!" I bellowed, throwing the mail into the air.

I had passed everything. Three C's and one B—in history. The Book must have liked my research essay. I was free!

Maybe.

Noting a C average in my graduating courses, universities wouldn't exactly be sending recruiting teams to sign me up, but—maybe.

Feeling pleased and a little like I had escaped the hangman, I bounced outside to wash the truck and remove the cap. I had to pick my parents up at the airport at nine fifteen. When I laid eyes on the dented hood and crumpled quarter panel all my good thoughts flew away. It was time to face the hangman after all.

I positioned the truck carefully in the airport parking garage, snugged tight against a wall so only the undamaged side was visible, and climbed out the passenger door. Stomach churning, I took the elevator to the departure level, wandered around until I realized I was in the wrong place, and rode the escalator to the arrivals level just in time to see Mom and Dad emerge from their gate.

We hugged hellos and after a few minutes' runaround—Mom's guitars had to be retrieved from the oversize baggage counter—we headed for the garage. I made all kinds of welcome-home noises, yapped away about Mom's flowers and even the weather as I dodged parent questions about what I had done for the last ten days to fill up my time. I caught Mom and Dad exchanging Who-is-this-babbling-idiot? looks. I walked ahead, pushing the luggage cart like a dutiful son.

"Why did you park here, like this?" Dad asked.

"It was really crowded when I came in," I said. "And by the way, I'll drive home. You look exhausted."

"No, I—"

"Here, I almost forgot," I cut in, and casually slipped my folded report card from my shirt pocket and handed it to my mother.

While they exclaimed their shared relief—did I hear a note of surprise in my father's words?—I stowed the luggage in the truck, pushed the cart to the side, and slid into the driver's seat.

"All aboard!" I called out enthusiastically. "Let's go!"

Mom got in first. As soon as Dad slammed the door I started the engine and drove down the ramp, chanting, "Please don't look at the hood," under my breath as I pulled to a stop under a blaze of amber light and paid the attendant.

The drive home was torture. My stomach pumped

out the acid. Every time Mom or Dad began to speak I expected a shriek of anger and despair. But nobody said a word about the bent metal in front of the windshield. Instead, my parents talked about my marks. Not exactly congratulatory, they seemed pleased in the reserved sort of way I was used to. You've done okay, Zack, but you could have done better—the kind of tone that robbed pleasure and replaced it with guilt. But the unexciting document had diverted their attention.

"Why don't you guys go on in," I said when I had parked in our driveway. "I'll take care of the luggage."

"My, my," Mom said. "You take a course in etiquette while we were gone?"

"Yup. Got an A, too."

"Hmm. I didn't see an A on that report card."

Mom walked toward the front door. Dad hauled the biggest suitcase from the truck.

"I guess tomorrow will be soon enough," he said. "I'm bushed."

I held a guitar case in each hand. "Huh?"

"To tell me about the truck."

"Look, let's get this straight. I admit I misled you. I confess I'm responsible for the truck. I'll pay for it. But I'm *not* sorry I went to Mississippi, so you may as well lay off the criticism."

The three Lanes sat around the kitchen table, an uneaten hamburger long since cold in front of each of us. Mom had performed her postgig rituals, visiting each of her plants inside the house and out to check on their health. She had done the laundry, pegged the clothes on the line in the yard. Her guitars had been unpacked and polished.

Dad's routine was to read and answer E-mail, open the paper mail and pay the bills, run the vacuum cleaner around the house. The morning inched by for me as I waited for the guillotine to drop.

Dad barbecued hamburgers as Mom complained about the smoke smelling up her laundry and, because the sun was high and hot he set up lunch in the kitchen. As soon as I said, "Pass the mustard," he nailed me.

So I told them.

"You *what*?" My mother had blown up as soon as she heard the word Natchez, and the further I waded into the story the more she fumed and raged, thumping her thighs with her fists.

I left out my tussle with the cops, the bigoted woman at the motel, the rednecks at the gas station. But I recounted the thunderstorm and fallen oak. I said I had met my grandfather, fished with him, gone to a funeral and a picnic. I explained why I had pretended to be someone else at first and how I discovered the reason my mother had nothing to do with him. I made clear the circumstances of my leaving Natchez. By the time I reached the end she was crying, hard and deep.

Relief was the main feeling that flowed in me by the time I was finished, but it wasn't the only one.

Dad had sat silently through it all, his face pale, and his eyes never left my mother's face.

"I've never felt so betrayed in my whole life," she whispered, wiping her eyes with a napkin. "And by my own son."

Her hands shook as she blew her nose. She gulped, choked back her crying, and cleared her throat.

It sounds strange, but the sight of her attempting to hold on to her grief made my heart ache for her, but I couldn't get hold of my thoughts, as usual. It's one thing to feel something and another to put the right words together so that the feelings come out under control, unmixed and unconfused. And so my response showed neither sympathy nor love, only anger.

"Mom, I didn't betray anybody. You made up your mind a long time ago that you never wanted to see your father again. Okay. But you didn't share the reason with me, did you? I'm not you. You don't have the right to decide for me anymore. I'm not a kid."

"Zack," Dad spoke for the first time. "You've got to understand how your mother feels."

"Dammit!" I exploded, pounding the table. The cutlery jumped and clinked; my mother flinched. "Why doesn't somebody try to understand how *I* feel for once?"

And I launched into a long rant, pulled out a lot of old tunes and played them one more time. How they had dragged me from my friends and neighborhood to a hick town. How they treated me like a five-year-old, forcing me to practically beg to use the truck, making me ask them for money because they wouldn't let me have a job—I was supposed to spend all my time studying. Nothing was decided by me. Nothing I did mattered. Unless I wrecked. Then it mattered.

My mind was a rage of contrary winds. I hated the weight of my father's disapproval. I hated the weight of my mother's pain. I hated myself for my inability to earn their pride.

But at the same time, I didn't want to be a dependent son any more, a kid yearning for a pat on the head, a teenager who screwed up, again, and waited for judgment. I wanted to be a person to them. Knowing I could never achieve what each of them had, never be their equal, I needed to be treated equally.

All this boiled and churned inside, and all that came out was anger. When I finally lost momentum and wound down, my mother said something peculiar.

"You always were contrary."

That threw me. I didn't follow. "I was what?"

"You never took music at school. You refused."

She sat there, head down, twisting the damp napkin to shreds. I looked at my father. Slowly, his eyebrows rose as if he expected me to say something, as if he thought I too knew what my mother meant.

"All that talent you have," she went on, her voice quavering, barely audible. "But you never took music in school. Just to be contrary."

Then I knew, and the realization was like a blow to the back of my head. She had concluded that I had avoided studying music to spite her. And now she thought my journey to find my grandfather was more of the same.

"Aw, Jesus," I moaned. "Mom—"

"Now don't you curse in this house, young man. You—"

"Etta," Dad said gently. "Let him talk."

"Mom, when I was a little kid," I said past the ache in my throat, "I wanted more than anything to be a musician like you. But I knew I could never be good enough. I couldn't even come close. I'd always be in your shadow, I'd let you down. I didn't stay away from music lessons to spite you. I stayed away because I was afraid I'd fail."

She looked up at me then. Amazement passed over her flushed features.

"But you *do* have the tal—"

"And my trip to Natchez? I didn't go to get back at

you, Mom. It was something I had to do, for *me*. I never knew or understood why you kept me from your—our—family."

In my mind, it was as if a cloud parted and the ideas I wanted to express became clearer.

"See, Mom, I've always felt like your part of me wasn't as important as Dad's part. I've always been proud to be a Jew, to be part of all our history and tradition. But I never felt that way about being African. I was never ashamed or anything—you and Dad made sure of that. It's just that I never had anything to build on, I wasn't connected to anything. Having black skin wasn't enough. I wanted to see where I came from, that was all.

"Now I know why you and your father are apart," I said bitterly. "He's no better than a redneck or a skinhead."

"I'm sorry you had to learn that, Zack," my mother said.

"But that's just it, Mom." I was calm now. But I wanted to make sure she knew. "I had to learn it for myself. But I also saw where our ancestors came from and I met some of our family. I like them. They're nice people. I liked Lucas too—"

Mom's eyes shot up when I called my grandfather by his first name, but that was what I had called him down there, and it seemed right.

"At first."

And then the doorbell rang.

"I'll get it," Dad said, clearly exasperated by the interruption.

My mother rose slowly from her chair, turned on the tap, and splashed water on her face, then used the dish towel to dry herself. She gathered the pile of shredded paper from the table and rolled it into a ball and put it in the garbage catcher under the sink. Then she sat down again.

I filled a glass with water and gulped it down like a marathon runner at the end of a race. Behind me I heard my father's voice.

"Someone to see you, Zack."

The Book looked wilted and hot in the kitchen doorway, wearing a shapeless dress plastered with big yellow sunflowers, and red plastic slip-ons, fanning herself with a large manila envelope. A few strands of jet-black hair stuck to the perspiration on her forehead.

"Er, hi," I blurted.

Dad introduced Song to my mother, who offered her a glass of lemonade, and we all gathered around the kitchen table, the Lanes fresh from an intense family skirmish and the Wicked Son's teacher—

ex-teacher, I corrected myself, since I was then officially a graduate. A visit from a teacher never meant anything good.

The three of them made small talk about the weather—they all agreed it certainly was hot and that the humidity sure made it seem hotter—and Song told Mom she had all three of her CDs and loved them, and I waited impatiently for Song to get to the point. My paranoia grew with each inane sentence they added to their conversation. Has Song come by to tell us that my history mark was an error, that I hadn't graduated after all?

My teacher finally got to me. "Zack, I've been trying to call you all week but your phone was out of order."

My father favored me with a sour look.

"And I've been so busy I couldn't come over until today," she went on in her usual breathless manner.

Mom shot me a What-Have-You-Done-Now? glance. I shrugged.

"Mr. and Mrs. Lane, as you know, Zack wrote a research paper to salvage his history mark. It was so good I took it to the county historical society—the Grand River and this area in particular are rich in history—well, I suppose everywhere is, isn't it?—and you must be fascinated, living on Pierpoint's very homestead, not to mention finding significant artifacts in your yard— Anyway, to get back to what I was saying—I'm always digressing—it drives my students crazy, doesn't it Zack?—no, don't answer that!— Anyway, on the basis of the paper, which was extremely well written and beautifully researched, they, the historical society, that is, want to offer Zack a history prize—it's only a hundred dollars, with a small plaque, but quite an honor—and a recommendation—which carries some considerable weight, by the way, and might just offset Zack's, um, not-so-high marks."

By the time The Book finally came up for air my parents were totally confused. So was I, but I thought I had heard the word *prize*.

"Ms. Song," Mom said, "I'm afraid I don't follow you."

"Oh, forgive me," my teacher said, flustered. "I haven't been very clear, have I? Zack has won a history prize."

"Research paper?" Dad said, catching up.

"I didn't tell them about it, Ms. Song," I explained.

"Why ever not?"

Because I was pretty certain I'd screw it up, I was tempted to answer. And if I did, it would be Zack the Lame Brain all over again.

"I wanted it to be a surprise."

"Wonderful," my mother muttered. "Another surprise."

"An award?" Dad latched on to another fact.

"Yes."

"And this historical society prize will help him get into a university?"

"It could."

Mom's eyebrows arched.

"Provided, of course, he takes his degree in history."

The Book sat back, crossed her hands on her lap, and smiled. She had delivered her good news.

Dad looked at me as if I had just burst through the door wearing a clown suit and holding a bunch of balloons on strings.

"Did you hear that, Etta?"

"But you haven't been accepted by a university yet," Mom said to me. Then a hint of a smile touched the corner of her mouth. "Or is there more?"

"No, Mom. I haven't been accepted."

"Zack's marks *are* a bit low," Song said for the second time—unnecessarily, I thought. "But, as I said, the historical society is full of people with, um, influence at the universities. Maybe it's a long shot but . . . well, we can hope."

I could have kissed her. She was determined to keep this news upbeat.

"What's this research paper about?" Dad asked.

Song beat me to it. She tapped the envelope. "It's right in here, Mr. Lane. And it's absolutely excellent. The historical society knows about Pierpoint, of course—so do I—but Zack's methodology, for a high-school student, is very fine. I knew he had it in him. But it took those artifacts he dug up in your yard to light a fire under him."

This time, both parents fixed me with a joint-effort stare.

"I was going to tell you about that too," I said weakly.

Mom rolled her eyes and let out a theatrical sigh. Dad just laughed.

Ms. Song saved me by jumping to her feet and pushing her chair tight to the table. "Well, must rush," she announced. And she did.

Jen flew in from Calgary the next day. As soon as I got her call, I drove over to her place to pick her up.

It was weird. We were shy with each other, as if we'd just met. I knew why I felt so strange. So much had happened, it seemed we'd been apart for a long time, but I couldn't figure out why she acted differently. Had she found another guy in Calgary?

I drove down to a quiet spot on the river and we spread a blanket out on the long grass where a big maple threw a pool of shade along the bank. The water purled by, brassy with afternoon sunlight, the way it had for thousands of years, and a pair of kingfishers took turns diving down and skimming along the surface.

Jen was as beautiful as ever. Out of the sunlight, her thick auburn hair took on a deeper shade. She was wearing a halter top and shorts that did nothing to hide her curves.

We sat silently for a few moments before she turned to me.

"Miss me?"

"I sure did."

"Prove it."

A few minutes later we unclinched, and I knew my fears about a cowboy lover out west were unfounded. Jen waded into the river up to her knees, far enough out that she was showered with sunlight. I pulled off my T-shirt, rolled it into a ball, and lay back, using the shirt as a pillow.

"I have something for you," Jen said. "A present."

"From Calgary?" Dammit, I thought, I should have brought her something from Mississippi.

"Nope. From right here in beautiful, boring Fergus. It's in my backpack, in a blue box."

I got to my knees and rummaged around in the pack until my fingers closed on a small gift box. I held it up.

"Well, open it, dopey."

I took off the lid and dropped it on the blanket, then removed a layer of white fluffy packing. What I saw knocked the breath out of me.

It had been cleaned and buffed so that the impurities contrasted sharply with the soft glow of the gold. A tiny ring had been skillfully soldered onto it and a gold chain passed through the ring so it could be hung around my neck.

I felt the water gather in my eyes, so that Pawpine's gold looked like a small moon in the palm of my hand. I heard Jen splash to shore. She knelt beside me and hugged me.

"I knew it almost killed you to part with it," she murmured. "So I phoned Mr. Piffard from Calgary the day after you left and asked him to let me buy it for you. He told me he realized you didn't really want to sell it and he was planning to keep it in the shop in case you came back for it. He came up with the idea of making a pendant out of it."

She gently took the nugget from my hand and unclasped the chain. Then she put it around my neck and refastened it. With her fingertips she brushed the water from my cheeks. She stared at the gold nugget, shaped like a musket ball, resting on the dark skin of my chest.

"God, that looks sexy," she whispered.

"Do you know what miscegenation is?"

"No. What?"

"Come here," I said.

The damp, loamy soil of the garden was cool under my bare feet, and as my hoe rose and fell, Pawpine's gold nugget bumped against my sweating chest. It was a few days after Jen had come home. Dad had quietly suggested that it might be a good idea to do some work in Mom's garden.

When all the soil had been loosened and banked and the dug-up weeds collected and tossed onto the compost heap, I leaned the hoe against the garage and swung my arms to shake out the stiffness between my shoulders, recalling the cop who had thrown me into the back of the cruiser and sprained my upper back.

Before I had gone outside into the garden, Mom had said, "How about showing me those things you dug up?"

That had been the first mention she had made about my project since Song's visit, so I guessed she'd been thinking over the last while. When I stepped into the cool of the kitchen she was sitting at the table with the document box, the white straps and neck ring before her and the essay in her hands.

She tamped the papers on the table to line them up. "Lawd, lawd, hee-ah come de fiel' han' want him sumpin cool to drink," she drawled.

"Not bad, Mom, not bad."

I popped a can of tonic water, leaned against the counter, and drained half the can in a few gulps.

"Your dad told me something last night that made me so mad I almost spit."

For my mother, that was strong language.

"We were talking about your . . . trip, and you know what he said? That he was proud of you."

I choked on the last mouthful of tonic water and coughed.

"Yeah," Mom said. "That's about how I reacted." She put down the paper and lifted Pawpine's neck iron, weighing it in her hands. "I can't say I agree, but I think I understand."

"What happened between you and Lucas, Mom? I know why you broke with him, but how come you never kept in touch with the others, like Cal and Ned? They seemed like nice guys. Do they think the way Lucas does?"

"No, I don't think so. But I was born and grew up in Chicago. My uncles and aunts stayed in Mississippi, so I didn't have much connection with them or my cousins, not even at Christmas, which your grandfather refused to celebrate anyway. I never knew my mother's family, really. She was an only child and her parents died before I was born.

"Your grandfather was always dead set against what he called the White Devil. You and I both know he had lots of reasons to be bitter, but he went too, too far. When I was grown and pretty much on my own I didn't see him too much, and after I met your father and we decided to be together, I phoned your grandfather back there in Chicago and told him I was getting married and planned to stay in Canada. He asked me about your dad, what he did for a living, things like that, then he said, 'Etta, for a girl who's getting married soon you don't sound very happy.' I said, 'Daddy, that's because I'm afraid to tell you something.'" Mom smiled and flushed a little.

"He thought I was pregnant. After I corrected him, he was silent for a long time and then he said, 'Etta, tell me it isn't what I think it is.' I told him, 'Daddy, I can't.'

"His voice came over all mean and low. He called me names, said I was no daughter of his if I went ahead. I said he had to accept your dad or lose me, I wasn't going to give Thom up. 'So be it,' he said, and hung up on me.

"Those were the last words I ever heard him say, 'So be it.'"

"Do you hate him, Mom?"

"I did for a long time. Now I just don't think of him anymore. He isn't part of my life. I've never regretted marrying your dad and I never will."

The iron clanked against the wooden tabletop when she put it down, lost in thought. I knew it was one of those times when her artistic mind was making connections only she could follow.

"You know, when you're angry, you have a look about you that reminds me of him." She shook her head. "He sure is a piece of work, that man."

At first I thought she meant my father.

"I hereby propose a toast," my father announced, looking faintly ridiculous as he stood at our formally laid dining-room table wearing a white apron with "DOWNE WITH IGNERENCE!" stenciled on the bib, a glass of cheap champagne in his hand.

The rest of us were dressed for the occasion. Mom wore a long roomy linen dress and, as always, hoop earrings; Jen was beautiful in a short skirt and silk blouse. I had on slacks and a white shirt. "You are not wearing cutoffs and a tank top to a graduation party," Jen had announced over my protests.

In the center of the table were two tall candles left over from Christmas/Hanukkah season, a smoking, mouthwateringly fragrant roast chicken on a cutting board, dishes of steaming roast potatoes, corn on the cob, peas, and, for Jen, who had decided last week that she was a vegetarian, a mammoth salad.

"To our honored guest," Dad bowed with mock formality, "Jen, student of . . . um . . ."

"Environmental science," Jen supplied with a giggle.

"Right, E.S., Innis College, University of Toronto. May you be the bane of polluting corporations and municipalities everywhere!"

We—Dad, Mom, Jen, and I—took sips of the bubbly stuff. Wine seldom made an appearance at my house, but this day was an exception, Dad had insisted. A graduation party of sorts, but mostly an induction party.

"Congratulations, Jen. Belated, but heartfelt all the same."

Mom and Jen clinked glasses.

"And to Zachariah, student of . . . er . . ."

"History, Dad. As if you forgot."

"Ah, yes, history, University College, University of Toronto."

Clink. We sipped again. The wine was sour and the bubbles went up my nose.

"Good luck to both of you," Mom said. After a moment she added, "Now, it's gift time."

My father reached under the table and handed a small box to Jen. She opened it and showed me a black fountain pen.

"Not a very imaginative graduation present, is it?" Mom said.

"It's lovely," Jen said. "Thank you, Mr. and Mrs. Lane. Look, Zack, my initials are engraved on the cap."

"Real scholars write with a fountain pen," Dad said, "not those plastic throwaways. And you being environmentally friendly and all . . ."

"Thanks," Jen repeated.

I could tell she was touched by their gift. I had given her mine the night before, a new backpack in heavy green nylon with lots of zippered compartments, straps, and buckles. Very romantic.

"Okay," I shouted, watching Jen turn the pen over and over in her hands. "My turn!"

I was in a pretty good mood. And a little scared, to be honest. In a couple of weeks I'd be leaving home to move into a residence. At long last I would escape the little town I used to hate but didn't anymore. I'd be back in the city, with the traffic, the smog, the noise, the energy that pulsed out of the pavement like heat on a July day; the movie theaters, the clubs, the stores and restaurants. I'd be starting a new life, as I had been yearning to do for so long. But I wondered if I was ready, if I would ever really be ready. True, Jen would be there. And that would help.

"Here you go," Dad announced.

Like a corny stage musician, he reached into his shirt pocket and slowly, humming a fanfare—if it was possible to hum a fanfare and make trumpet sounds through your lips, my father could do it—he drew out a key. He then held it between thumb and index finger, showed it to all of us, individually, as if he was about to make it disappear, then casually tossed it onto the tablecloth in front of me.

It was the key to the Toyota.

"You're kidding," I murmured.

"Nope. Your mom and I want you to have the truck. After all, you've put your mark on it, in a manner of speaking."

Mom threw back her head and laughed. Her earrings jumped and swung. A week before, my parents had come home one night with a used—"previously experienced"—Jeep Cherokee—part of the image of the rural resident, I guessed, and they had built racks for the interior to hold Mom's instruments and gear. I had hoped I could take the Toyota to Toronto, but I figured the odds were against me.

"Thanks, Mom and Dad, this is great."

"The truck is from your dad," Mom said right away.

"Oh."

Confused, I watched as she got up and walked into her studio. A moment later she returned with one of her guitars. It was her favorite, an old acoustic six-string with a smooth mellow sound that perfectly complemented her voice. Awkwardly, she laid the instrument in my lap.

"Give us a few riffs," she said.

Stirred by an unfocused excitement, I strummed a few complicated blues chords she had taught me not long before. I had been practicing them every day.

"Not bad. Maybe you better take that old thing with you when you go to school so you can practice some more."

"Mom, you mean—"

"You take music lessons when you get to the city, son." And she leaned down and kissed me, holding me tight to her body for a few seconds before she sat down again.

I cradled the guitar, ran my hand up and down the neck, admiring the pearl finish of the tuning pegs, the grain in the polished wood of the box, the area beneath the hole worn to a lighter shade by strumming fingers. I recalled the times when I was so small I could hardly hold the guitar. I would play with it when Mom was out of the apartment and Dad preoccupied with his work. It was only now, as I held it, my hands leaving barely visible smudges in the waxed finish, that I realized she must always have known I had held it and tried to make music.

I heard the doorbell ring as I examined the worn spots between the frets.

"I'll get it," Jen said.

I looked up at my mother. "Mom, I don't know what to say. Thanks—"

From behind me I heard, "Is this the Lane residence?" The voice seemed somehow familiar.

My mother did not acknowledge my words. A look of horror struck her face, and her wine glass, which hung suspended from the fingertips of both her hands, dropped. The stem split away and fragments of glass and foaming champagne blossomed up from the table.

"Oh, my Lord," she whispered.

I turned in my chair, the recognition of the voice hitting me exactly at the moment my eyes took in the figure at the door.

He leaned on his cane in the doorway, his free hand clutching and working the hem of his black suit jacket. He had on a white shirt and a wide red tie even I knew was way out of style.

Jen stood with her hand on the doorknob, staring past Lucas at me, her face clouded with confusion. Dad looked at my mother with his head tilted to one side the way he did when he was surprised. The wet mark on the tablecloth spread slowly outward, unnoticed by my mother, whose fingertips pressed her cheeks beside her open mouth.

"Hello, Etta," my grandfather's deep voice broke the spell. "Hello, Zack."

Dad's glance switched from Mom to the stranger at the door as he tried to put the pieces together.

"Is this who I think it is?" he asked my mother.

When she spoke, her words were as hard as stone. "What are you doing here, Lucas?"

Outside the window I could see a red and yellow taxi in the driveway and the rumble of its motor rode on the silence in the house. Lucas had told the driver to wait, I saw, because he expected to be shunned and he would have to leave again, knew he would be turned away, knew he deserved to be.

"You must be Thom," he said.

"Yes."

"Zack favors you, around the chin."

Mississippi was far away, but Lucas's mellow drawl brought it all back to me—the slow warm water of the bayou, moss-hung live oaks in the yard, the hot, hot air so thick with humidity it was like a second skin.

"Really," my father said icily.

Jen had come and stood by my chair. "What's going on?" she whispered.

"He's my grandfather."

"You mean the one who—" she blurted, her skin flushing immediately after the words left her mouth. "I'd better take off, Zack."

"You stay right where you are," my mother commanded. "There's no need for *you* to go."

Which made Jen, I could see, want to leave more than ever.

Now that my grandfather and mother were in the same room, the resemblance between them was obvious—the facial features, the slender form, the proud bearing, even though Lucas stooped a little. But where Mom's jaw was set and her eyes crackled with fire, Lucas looked tired and thoughtful, and the way he gripped the head of his cane hinted at his discomfort. No one in the house wanted him there, and he knew it.

"Etta, I'd 'preciate it if you'd hear me out. Got a taxi waiting out yonder. Won't take long."

"You said all you had to say a long time ago, old man," my mother hissed.

He nodded his head twice. "Won't take long," he repeated. "I come a long way to see you."

My father, who was usually Mr. Good Host, didn't say a word. He knew this was Mom's call, and he waited. We all waited. The silence and tension grated on my nerves. Jen began to chew a fingernail, a pained Get-me-out-of-here look on her face.

Why was my grandfather here? I wondered. Had he found out he was going to die and decided to make peace with his daughter? Not likely, given his attitude toward people he called the whites. Did he need money? Was he in some kind of trouble? He had relatives around Natchez. Why come here?

The thought of his—and my—relatives brought to my mind something I had been trying to forget: the look on his face that morning in his yard when I had told him who I was and he had said he hadn't known he had a grandson. And the words I had spat back at him.

"Mom, Dad," I said. "Couldn't you at least hear what he has to say?"

My mother sat as stiff and unyielding as an oak plank at one end of the table. Broken glass littered the stained tablecloth in front of her but she made no move to pick up the pieces. I studied my father's face. He knew he was the "cause" of the break between my mother and Lucas. He'd been called names on the street all his life; he'd read and seen the racist no-minds in print and in person. Lucas was just one more. Dad could handle his hatred. It was the effect on my mother that worried him.

"It's all right with me," Dad said. "Etta?"

Mom didn't flinch, didn't utter a sound.

Dad handed me a few bills. "Zack," he said, "go out and pay off that cab."

Lucas limped to the table, his cane tapping on the hardwood floor, and took a seat between my mother and me. He sat straight, both hands resting on the top of his cane. He wouldn't take his eyes off my mother. For her part, she refused to meet his gaze. She looked away through the door to the kitchen, as if she had something on the stove and feared it would boil over.

"Etta," Lucas began, almost whispering, "my old friend Ray passed on not long ago." His Adam's apple rose and fell. "And it got me thinkin' about things. I guess when you get old, when your friends pass, you look back on your life. Kind of take stock, like. I began to wonder if I haven't come up short."

My mother continued to look away, but her face softened a little.

"Then Zack here come down to my place. To see me, I reckon. But before I knew who he was, I thought to myself, there's a fine young man would make any parent proud. Any grandparent too. And when he finally told me he was my grandson, and I learned he was named after my daddy . . ."

He trailed off, swallowed hard, and got himself under control again.

"I . . . I've suffered a lotta hate in my life, and a long time ago I learned to fight that hate by turning it back against them that held me down, denied me things because I'm black, and against the system that let 'em do it. It was the only defense I had. But, Etta, I let it poison me. I'm not makin' excuses for myself, mind you. I'm tryin' to explain."

Only then did my mother face him, as if to confirm the terrible error and the judgment he heaped on himself.

"Etta, after all these years, I know an apology don't mean nothin'. But I done you a world of wrong, and I'm sorry for it."

Lucas turned to my father. "Sir," he said, almost formally, as if he had rehearsed his lines again and again, "I never met you before today, and I done you a deep wrong too."

My mother let the words lie a moment, then she spoke, every word sharp as a knife. "Lucas, do you remember what you said to me when I told you I was going to marry Thom? You said I was a traitor to my race, that any black woman who would take up with a white man was trash. You didn't care that Thom is a wonderful man. You didn't want to know. You did to Thom and me what you hated others for doing to you. Now you're sorry," she said with contempt.

Lucas took the assault straight on, with his chin up. I had to admire the way he kept his dignity.

"I sat down a dozen times to write," he said. "But words on paper wasn't enough; they was too easy. Zack come a long way to Mississippi. After he left I tried to reason out why he had come down all that way. Then I remembered that song of yours he sang for us all, and I read that school project he left me and

I knew. I told myself, if he could come to Natchez and face me, I had to come and face you."

My mother turned to me and in her face I saw something I couldn't name. Lucas got to his feet and let out a sigh.

"Zachariah," he said, "I'm sorry we never got to know each other better."

I didn't answer him. I didn't know what to say.

"Now," he continued, "I'd 'preciate it if y'all'd telephone for a taxi to carry me back to the airport."

I thought for a moment. "I guess I could take you," I offered.

"I'll come with you," Jen said.

It would be nice, I guess, to say that it was a Disney-type ending, that we all fell into one another's arms weeping and laughing at the same time, that forgiveness flowed like the river at the foot of our yard, that we sat down together in fellowship and continued the graduation party. But the wounds ran deep in all of us, and the interrupted meal cooled uneaten on the table.

No one asked Lucas to stay. I'm certain that he would have refused anyway. He had come north to start the healing, to make a beginning, and although my feelings for him were a long way from positive, I respected him for his courage. It's a lot harder to fix something than it is to break it.

I know that my parents felt the same. Before Lucas left our house, my father shook his hand firmly and my mother asked him to give her his address and phone number.

"Maybe I'll call you some time," she said.

We got to the airport in lots of time for his flight but he asked us not to wait with him. He shook hands with Jen and me and limped through the security doors and disappeared.

Jen and I were silent for most of the way home. I was thinking—like a historian already, I guess—how one person's actions can ripple through the years and affect so many others, and how most of the time the results of what we do can't be predicted or known. A long, long time before, a lonely old man had buried a document box on his farm by the shore of the Grand River. The box lay in the earth for more than 150 years, until its discovery forged a chain of events that drew another old man from Mississippi to the same farm so that he could make a new connection to his daughter and her family. I was the link between the two men. One of them I admired; the other, who should have been closer to me because he was my grandfather, I didn't. Pawpine had never given up, but Lucas had. He had let hatred wrestle him down and defeat him. But in coming all the way from Natchez, maybe he had begun to stand up again.

APPENDIX

South on '61
Words by William Bell
Music by Dylan Bell
Slow, Delta-blues style
voice
guitar
1. Well, I'm
2.
hea-din' south— on six-ty-one—
Cot-ton broke— my daddy's back
G7
I'm go-in' home a-
It broke his dad-dy's
gain
too
C7
G7
guitar play riff between stanzas
But Chi-
Back to where— I came from
cago's long— as-sembly lines
— back to all the
are si-lent as a
pain
tomb
My—
They
lea-vin' was so desp'rate
drove him back down sixty-one
to Coda
G7

my co-min' home's the
with nothin' but the
Same
blues
Oh, Mama, Why'd you leave me?
Why you been gone so
long?
It's
now that I most need you —
to say where I be—
long
I'm
hea-din' back down Sixty-one —
with no-thin' but this

Song

Ol'

Six-ty one — she led us north to jobs, pros-pe-ri-ty — and

C7 C7

gave us fro-zen ghettos and a life of mi-ser-y — she

Bb7 Bb7

runs in two di-rec-tions, and nei-ther one is

A7

D.S. al Coda

free. Well, I'm

G7

Coda

freely... a tempo

My co-min' home's the same:

Ab7 G7

AUTHOR'S NOTE

With the exception of people and events taken from the historical record, this is a work of fiction. Any resemblance between my characters and real persons, living or dead, is entirely coincidental.

Richard Pierpoint did exist and ended his days on the homestead he and a friend had cleared from the bush on the banks of the Grand River at present-day Fergus, Ontario. I have tried to render his story accurately, but took one small liberty: As far as I know, he didn't bury anything on his farm.

ACKNOWLEDGMENTS

As always, thanks are due to John Pearce, who kept the faith when I had almost lost it; to Ting-xing Ye for encouragement and for help with the manuscript; to my children, Dylan, Megan, and Brendan, for reading and responding to the early drafts.

I appreciate the assistance of Wayne Allen, history teacher at Orillia Collegiate; Ian Easterbrook and Bonnie Callan, archivists at the Wellington County Museum and Archives; and the support of the Ontario Arts Council.

I first heard of Richard Pierpoint (alias Pawpine) from the song "Pawpine" written by James Gordon of the folk band Tamarack. It can be found on the CD *On the Grand* (FE1421CD), copyright Folk Era Productions, Inc.